SADDLEBAG DISPATCHES MAGAZINE PRESENTS

UNDER ❧ THE ❧ HOT PRAIRIE SUN

BLOOD, DUST, AND DESTINY ON THE PLAINS

Saddlebag Dispatches, LCC
A Subsidiary of Oghma Communications
Bentonville, Arkansas
www.saddlebagdispatches.com

Under a Hot Prairie Sun: Blood, Dust, and Destiny on the Plains
Description: First Edition | Bentonville: Saddlebag Dispatches, 2025
Identifiers: ISBN: 979-8-89299-049-3 (trade paperback)| ISBN: 979-8-89299-050-9 (eBook)
FICTION/Westerns | FICTION/Action & Adventure |
FICTION/Thrillers/Historical

Trade Paperback edition April, 2025

Cover Design and Interior Design by Casey W. Cowan
Editing by Anthony Wood, Dennis Doty & Don Money

SADDLEBAG DISPATCHES MAGAZINE PRESENTS

UNDER THE HOT PRAIRIE SUN

BLOOD, DUST, AND DESTINY ON THE PLAINS

Breaking Through the Line by Charles Schreyvogel

TABLE ⚙ CONTENTS

The Scalp Lock by Alfred Jacob Miller

LIST *of* ILLUSTRATIONS

Bucking On a Dime by W.H.D. Koerner

PREFACE

PRAIRIE! The very sound of the word conjures images of never-ending wagon trails across sodded, treeless ground. It's where men, women, and families either survived or thrived on their trek west—no in between. Stories of the plains bring to mind men and women battling the elements, hostile outlaws and Native Americans, and the unending search for a new life. All set out to find it. Many fell short of the prize.

In *Under the Hot Prairie Sun: Blood, Dust, and Destiny,* you'll come face to face with that undying, ever-hopeful American spirit. It drove the best of who the East could offer to face insurmountable struggles that left only those with the determined will to become more in the great American West.

Traipse alongside award winning authors Regina McLemore, Kevin Brown, Blanche Deschain, Rick Sapp, Lee Clinton, and Del Garrett, who will draw you across the prairie into tales that won't let you leave the campfire except for another cup of hot coffee.

Follow a man into town seeking only rest and a shot of whiskey but is pestered by a drunken bully until there is no alternative but to fight him. Trek along with a guilt-ridden bounty hunter who can find no peace in this life, even with weapons named Sinner and Unforgiven held in each hand. Scrap alongside a journalist who wants to hunt antelope but bags a size-twenty sweetheart. Ride along with a newlywed couple who discover that the hardships they face on the trail traveling to their new home make their marriage even stronger.

Find your best blanket to ward off the evening chill and settle in as the coyotes begin to howl, because you're in for a treat taking the trail *Under the Hot Prairie Sun: Blood, Dust, and Destiny* with some of the best authors in western short story writing.

—Anthony Wood
Managing Editor, *Saddlebag Dispatches*
March 3, 2025

SADDLEBAG DISPATCHES MAGAZINE PRESENTS

UNDER ✥THE✥ HOT PRAIRIE SUN

BLOOD, DUST, AND DESTINY ON THE PLAINS

Night Herder by Frank Tenney Johnson

A SHRED ❦ HUMAN DECENCY

BRUCE HARTMAN

THEY CALLED HIM the Bard of the Badlands because he liked to sing cowboy songs and tell stories about the old days. You could usually find him squatting on a crate outside the feed store, chewing tobacco, and whittling sticks down to nothing. For us boys, listening to him was a real treat, but our folks warned us to stay away from him. He'd ridden the cattle trails and gambled in the saloons and had a few brushes with the law back when there wasn't much law to brush up against. He had no end of stories. His usual fee for telling one was a glass of whiskey, but for us boys, it was on the house. One afternoon, while we crowded around him, he told us the tale of a bad man who followed a river that went nowhere and was tamed by a coyote.

YOU BOYS ARE too young to remember Tom McGuinness who lost his way in the Humboldt Sink. First, I better tell you what that is. Rivers generally run toward the ocean or a bigger river—picking up water as they go. But west of Elko, Nevada, there's a river that's pointed in the wrong direction. If you follow it downstream, it gets narrower and narrower with less and less water in it until finally it flat-out disappears. Sinks into the sand in the middle of the desert. And, if you'd been following it hoping to get to California, like some people did in the early days, that's where you'd end up. Thirsty, starving, burned to a crisp, and wishing you'd stayed home.

That's pretty much what happened to Tom McGuinness. He lived in Elko, and by all accounts, he was a very bad man. He robbed a bank and shot two tellers and three old ladies who happened to be in the bank. A posse caught him and brought him back to Elko for trial, and he never denied what he done. The jury had no sympathy for him and took about five minutes to convict him. "Thomas McGuinness," the judge said when it came time for sentencing, "you are a cold-blooded killer lacking even a shred of human decency or any other redeeming qualities. I sentence you to hang at 12:00 noon on Saturday the tenth of July."

In the next few days, Tom McGuinness had plenty of time to think, which was something he'd never done much of. He'd always figured he would end up on the wrong end of a rope, but what the judge said about him lacking even a shred of human decency was like a slap in the face. Was it true? Well, maybe so. He must've admitted to himself that he'd never done anything but prey on other people, never helped anybody out, never even rescued a cat in a tree, and when he tried to think of some redeeming qualities he probably drew a blank. Still, to have that insult added to his sentence stuck in his craw. It wasn't right belittling a man like that.

The night before his scheduled hanging, the deputy accidently left his cell door ajar, and he slipped outside. He headed west along the river, which seemed wide enough that it must be going somewhere. After the first day, he fell in with an old prospector named Hank walking alongside a burro loaded with food and water and prospecting gear. Hank was a friendly old coot with bright blue eyes and a grizzly beard who liked to talk to pass the time. It would have been easy enough to kill him and steal his burro and supplies, and naturally, the thought crossed McGuinness's mind. But he told himself that Hank could be useful to him. He seemed to know the trail, but that turned out to be an illusion. The river got narrower and narrower as they followed it into the desert country. Then it split into a dozen branches. Each carried a thin trickle of salty brown water until it sank into the ground. If there was a trail in that wasteland, neither of them could find it. Looking ahead, they saw nothing but shimmering white sand, mirages that looked like faraway mountains, and a vast graveyard of sun-bleached skeletons and skulls, ribcages of oxen and horses and Conestoga wagons, and everything those wagons had brought there, trunks and chests, bolts of cloth, furniture, musical instruments, strewn and mingled in the windblown sand. Under the blistering sun, there wasn't a speck of shade or a blade of grass. A dozen buzzards spiraled over them high in the sky.

"Tracks in the sky," Hank said.

"What do you mean?" McGuinness asked.

"Somebody could follow us by watching them buzzards. They been trailing us for a week. 'Awaiting the will of God,' the Mexicans say."

They didn't have long to wait. After two more days, the food and water ran out and the burro breathed its last. "Let's leave him here in the valley of bones," Hank said. "Maybe the buzzards'll eat their fill and leave us alone."

They left the burro where it fell, taking only their rifles, packs, and a thin blanket each.

"Better bring the shovel, too," Hank said. "We'll be needing that soon. One of us anyway."

Two days later, they could hardly lift their feet to walk. They crawled into a dry gulch speckled with sagebrush and prickly pear where an overhang offered a sliver of shade from the afternoon sun. They avoided looking at the sky, but when McGuinness finally did, he saw the buzzards again circling overhead. From across the gulch, about fifty yards away, a lone coyote watched them huddle in the overhang. It was the first living thing they'd seen—besides the buzzards—since the burro died.

"It was the buzzards led her to us," Hank said.

"How do you know that coyote's a female?"

"I can just tell. You wait till tonight. You'll see."

And that night, after the moon rose in the east, the coyote yodeled out the loveliest song McGuinness had ever heard. He named her Jenny, after Jenny Lind the Swedish nightingale.

When morning came, Hank was cold and stiff as a cedar post. McGuinness filched the money and tobacco from his pockets and decided not to bury him. Better to leave him stretched out in full view to keep the buzzards off his trail for a couple of days. He pulled off the old man's boots and muttered a curse against the buzzards.

Across the gulch, the coyote sat on her haunches, tail switching from side to side, and watched him patiently. She tracked us by the buzzards, he thought, just like the old man said. He considered shooting her, but when he reached for his rifle, she ducked out of sight. The sun blazed like an inferno, and he was weak from thirst and starvation. He stood up and walked a few steps and collapsed in the sand. When he looked up, the buzzards were already swooping down and pecking at Hank's face and eyes. For some reason—he couldn't have explained it to himself—McGuinness felt a surge of outrage at this sight. He hardly knew Hank and might have killed him if he'd a reason, but the sight of the old prospector being dismembered and eaten by buzzards was too much. He raised his rifle and fired. One of the birds exploded in a mess of blood and feathers and careened into the gulch. The others squawked and flew away.

When McGuinness stood up, he glanced into the gulch and instead of what he expected—the buzzard's shattered carcass in the sand among the sagebrush and cactus—he saw the coyote trotting off with the dead bird in her mouth. Hungry as he was, the idea of eating a buzzard revolted him. "You can have it, Jenny," he called out to her. "You can have all the dead buzzards you want."

His most pressing need was for water. Without water he wouldn't last another day. Kneeling in the gulch with his knife, he cut a cactus into pieces—snagging hundreds of tiny spines in his hands as he worked. Ignoring the pain, he stripped off his shirt and squeezed the juice of the prickly pear into it one drop at a time. When the shirt was soaked, he wrung it out in a tin bowl he carried in his pack. After an hour, he had filled the bowl with a cup of cactus juice which he poured down his throat. It burned going down and made his stomach curl up like a fist. His hands were swollen and throbbing, and he felt feverish and faint. With his last ounce of strength, he wrapped his blanket around himself and fell asleep.

He dreamed that he died and went to hell. In his dream, he lay stretched out in a burning lake. The sizzling lakebed was as hot as a skillet. Fire rained down on him from a flaming sky. He writhed and cried out in an agony that would never end.

After what seemed an eternity, he woke himself up vomiting and gagging, spewing the bitter cactus juice on the sand, delirious, shivering, and gasping for breath. When he'd mustered enough strength to lift his head, he realized that his nightmare of hell had been an exact replica of the landscape around him. No, not quite exact. He realized the buzzards were back—a dozen of them circled impatiently over his head. "That's a good sign," he told himself, recalling something Hank had said. "It means you ain't dead yet."

The coyote—or was it a hallucination of the coyote—eyed him curiously from about fifty feet away. She raised a front paw and turned to the side, ran a few paces, stopped, and looked back pointing with her ears. Was she trying to lead him away? He struggled to his feet and followed her as she trotted down the gulch, stopping every fifty feet to make sure he was behind her. At last, she arrived at a depression crowded with sagebrush and yucca and various kinds of cactus and marked on one edge by a heap of sand that looked like a recent excavation.

McGuinness staggered to the heap and looked down into a hole dug in the sand. There was mud on the bottom. Not water, just mud, but it was wet enough to strain through his shirt as he'd done with the cactus juice. In fifteen minutes, he'd filled his bowl with slightly muddy water. He guzzled it and strained out another bowlful and repeated this until he'd slaked his thirst. He was so desperate to drink that he all but forgot about the coyote.

But she hadn't forgotten him. She squatted not more than twenty paces away swishing her tail from side to side. Her straw-yellow eyes glistened with expectation. He realized that she expected a drink of water, too. He strained out another bowlful and set it on the sand. "I guess you've earned it," he said as he stepped back to let her drink. "But don't get any ideas in your head. The next time I have my rifle handy, I've a mind to shoot you."

As she stared back at him, he thought he saw a glimmer of reproach in her eyes. "I shot that buzzard for you this morning," he explained, "and now you've found me this water, so we're quits. But a man's got to eat."

That night after the moon rose silver in the sky he listened to the coyote's solitary song. There was a note of sadness in that song, but was it the coyote's sadness he wondered, or his own? This was the last night his Jenny would sing—or, if he didn't find something to eat, the last night he would hear it. Which would it be? His hunger filled the whole space between him and the stars.

The next morning, before he opened his eyes, he knew he had to kill the coyote. "The Indians eat dogs," he told himself. "I could do a lot worse." But before he could stand up with his rifle, the coyote trotted up with something in her mouth and dropped it at his feet. It was a small brown rat about the size of his hand twitching in its death agonies.

"You expect me to eat this?"

Of course she did. Kangaroo rats were one of her favorite delicacies.

McGuinness did a quick calculation. If he killed the coyote, he might live off the meat for three or four days, but if he kept her alive and she brought him a rat every day, he could hang on until he found his way out of the desert. Rat meat was better than prison food and worlds better than what he would taste on the gallows.

He built a fire and skinned and roasted the rat. As he ate, the coyote gnawed on the skin and helped herself to one of old Hank's leather boots. After so much meat eating, they were both as thirsty as the dickens. He picked up his tin bowl and led the coyote back to the mud hole where they had found water the day before. It was as dry as a bone. The coyote trotted away and led him to a deeper hole near the mouth of the gulch. In this one, he could see his face reflected up from a pool of clear water—within easy reach for him but too far down for the coyote. He dipped his bowl in, swallowed a long draft, and filled it again for his little friend.

The next morning, he woke up to find a rattlesnake coiled around his neck. Its castanets chattering, its serpent's tongue flickered in front of his eyes. He felt the iron hand of death choking off his breath and sinking its claws into his heart. If he'd known any prayers, he would have said one. Out of the corner of one terrified eye, he glimpsed the coyote studying him with cheerful curiosity from about four feet away. Her pink tongue lolled between white glistening teeth. Easy now, he told her with his eyes. Don't do anything that'll scare it. He knew he'd be a dead man if he moved a muscle. Maybe she'd like that, he thought, noticing the savage gleam in her eyes. Maybe she'd like to see the rattler kill me so she can feast on what's left over.

Suddenly, the coyote sprang forward and snagged the hissing snake just back of the head as it waved past McGuinness's eyes. She clenched it tightly and snapped it away from his face before it could bite him. Without changing his position, he reached in his belt and found his knife. He sliced through the rattler's neck and cut off its head—which the coyote quickly tossed aside. Then she snatched up the rest of the snake and loped away with it. But after a few paces she stopped, turned around, dropped the rattler on the ground, and gazed back at McGuinness with a silent plea he had no trouble understanding.

"I guess you want it cooked," he said. "Well, so do I. Let's get a fire going and cook up a nice rattler breakfast."

As they crouched at the edge of the gulch eating their roasted rattlesnake, McGuinness asked himself why the coyote had saved his life. "It can't be human decency," he reasoned, "because a coyote ain't human. And no human I've ever known would've done such a thing."

For another week, he and the coyote pooled their talents in the hunt for food and water. They took turns decoying their prey, drawing them out, and killing them—always dividing the bounty equally. McGuinness stood in awe of the coyote's cunning and resourcefulness. To confuse the prey she played dead, ran in circles chasing her tail, leaped in the air as if it were all a game. She could disappear into the landscape and reappear fifty yards away. In the early morning light, she took on the shape of a rock or a cactus. At noontime with her back to the blinding sun, she hid in plain view—visible and invisible at the same time and ranging unpredictably over the desert like the spirit of creation itself.

The wildlife—rats, lizards, prairie dogs—grew more plentiful as they came closer to civilization. They found patches of grass, wind-twisted trees, and the spoor of horses and sheep, and then one morning, cresting a low rise, they discovered a small sheep ranch half-hidden in sagebrush and pinyon pine. Behind the sheepherder's cabin stood a sheep pen, a horse corral, and a fenced-in yard bustling with chickens. McGuinness raised his rifle and clicked off the safety.

The sheepherder, gray-bearded old timer with steely blue eyes, wearing a battered hat and clothes patched together from buckskin and other animal hides stepped out from behind a pinyon pine twenty yards away. It startled him to see McGuinness standing there with his rifle raised. He stumbled backwards into a gopher hole, twisting his ankle, and went down on all fours. He tried to stand up, but the ankle buckled, and he collapsed back down in the dirt. He raised his head and peered warily at the intruder.

McGuinness could easily have shot him, and for a long moment he thought about it. After all, he was a convicted murderer sentenced to hang—with all the freedom that entails—nothing he did could have altered his fate. In the cabin, there was food, water, and a bed, behind it a horse in the corral, sheep in the sheep pen, and chickens in the chicken yard. He glanced down at the coyote who sat watching him. Her tail swishing. Her head slightly tilted. A sparkle of puzzlement in her straw-yellow eyes. It was as if she could read his mind and had grave misgivings about what he was contemplating. She must have known that the sheepherder was of his own kind, and she couldn't imagine that he could shoot the man. Oddly enough, he felt the same way. His step faltered as he lowered his rifle and called out to the sheepherder.

The sheepherder looked up at him and broke into a smile. "I saw the buzzards and figured I'd be meeting somebody at least half dead."

"Tracks in the sky," McGuinness mumbled, noticing the buzzards circling overhead for the first time.

"You look like you've been through hell. Can you give me a hand? If you're hungry, there's plenty of grub inside."

McGuinness stooped down, picked the old man up, and slung one arm across his shoulder. Then he carried him step-by-step across the rocky hillside toward the cabin.

"I'm much obliged, my friend," the sheepherder said. "It's mighty decent of you."

As he led the sheepherder to the cabin, Tom McGuinness tried to come to grips with his sudden loss of nerve. Ten days in the desert with that coyote had transformed him into something he didn't recognize. What had happened to him? And, what would become of him now that he was back among his own kind? He felt a strange lump in his throat as if something was stuck in it.

He glanced back around, but the coyote was nowhere to be seen. Indifferent to human affairs, she had ducked out of sight when he bent down to help the sheepherder.

I reckon all she could think about was how to get into that chicken yard.

———————◆◆◆———————

—Bruce Hartman has been writing fiction for over fifty years. His current project is a trilogy of novels set in Colorado, Montana, and Oklahoma, focusing on the great cattle boom of the 1870s and 1880s, its catastrophic collapse in the Big Die-Up of 1886-87, and the impact of those events on the men and women who built their lives around the cattle business, as well as on the native people in the region. Bruce traces his roots to the West and lived for many years in Colorado. Currently he divides his time between Colorado and Pennsylvania. He is a member of Western Fictioneers and an Associate Member of Western Writers of America.

Prospector and Donkey by W.H.D. Koerner

BADGES AND BULLETS

DEL GARRETT

PACO LOPEZ SAT motionless in his saddle and looked at the cloudless Texas sky above him and down at the dry, grassy embankment beneath him where a rider sat on a broad-chested Appaloosa. The man shook his head, grinned, then spat out a wad of tobacco at Paco's quarter horse, making him jerk and whinny.

Paco sat still. Strands of leather cut deep into his wrists but not as tight, he thought, as the latigo noose around his neck. Cowboys on either side of him hooted and hollered as they jostled Ol' Blaze, making the animal step this way and that. A few of them reached out to cuff Paco's face as they swung past him. They're just funnin' me, Paco thought. They ain't ready to see me swing yet—I hope.

Arley Wade, top hand for the MacCullaugh Ranch, eased his Appaloosa up close and looked Paco in the eye.

"Well, Mex, you ready to die?"

"Oh, no, *señor,* not really. But like the Indians say, 'It's a good day to die.'"

Wade took off his brown slouch hat. He pulled a soiled, red bandana from his back pocket and wiped it across his forehead. The bandana picked up what perspiration was there, which hadn't already made a dark band around the crown of his hat. Wade shoved the rag back in his pocket and grinned at Paco. His mouth ran wide showing a row of overly large front teeth heavily stained from tobacco juice. "If you say so, jackass." Wade raised his hat high and leaned out of his saddle so he could swat Ol' Blaze on the rump.

"Hold it right there!" The voice came from less than ten feet away. Wade turned his head and saw a double-barrel shotgun being aimed at him. Behind the shotgun was a face he knew well and a badge that glistened in the high-noon sunlight.

"Why, hello, Sheriff Clayborn. Caught us a steer rustler here. We'uz just about to send him to his just rewards."

"Ain't gonna be no hanging today, Wade. Cut him loose."

"Oh, I don't think we can do that, Sheriff." Wade moved his horse between the sheriff's shotgun and the rear end of Paco's horse. "You forget, you ain't got no jurisdiction way out here."

"This shotgun gives me all the jurisdiction I need. Now, cut him loose." The sound of both hammers being cocked on the shotgun echoed across the open plains. The only other sound came from the slow gurgle of a stream winding lazily along across MacCullaugh land.

The sound of the hammers locking back ran through Arley Wade's body like an icicle down the back of his shirt. The sound made him pull back on his reins causing his horse to nudge Ol' Blaze and start him forward, stretching Paco's neck tighter than before. Paco dug his heels gently into the horse's shoulders and held fast in the saddle. His neck turned white where the rope dug in, and his face turned a shade or two bluer.

"Mister MacCullaugh ain't gonna like this, you butting in on his business." Wade spoke harshly. The other cowhands sat nervously in their saddles. Their hands moved ever so slightly toward their six-shooters but stopped before drawing their guns. Sheriff Clayborn took notice of their movements but never let his gaze drift away from the foreman.

"I don't give a hang what Mister MacCullaugh likes or doesn't like when it comes to murder. And, Wade, you better tell your boys here that if their hands get any closer to their guns I'm just going to squeeze both triggers on this scattergun and drop it while I draw my own pistol. They might get me, but you'll be in hell thirty seconds before I get there. Understand?"

"Boys, he ain't kidding. Ease back a bit. We'll catch this no-good Mex some other time when Mister Hero ain't around to save him."

In a gallop, the MacCullaugh men hurried away over a ridge. Sheriff Clayborn uncocked his 12-gauge and eased his horse up alongside Ol' Blaze. He drew a Bowie knife from his belt and severed the rope just above Paco's head.

"Feel better?"

"Si, mi amigo. You came along just in time. I buy you a drink, maybe?"

"Let's get off MacCullaugh land first. He's got a lot of men, and it wouldn't be smart to hang around."

"Si, mi compadre."

The sheriff and Paco wasted no time heading for town.

On the rise above them, Arley Wade sat on his horse and fumed as he watched the two men ride away.

"Yore time's a-coming, Clayborn. I ain't forgetting, and I ain't forgiving. You and me are gonna tie up again soon. Real soon!"

———————————————

TEXAS RANGER BILL Shackley drew his pistol and fired, hitting Mayor Grant Colby in his left leg. The mayor, having killed a drifter in a rigged poker game two weeks before, held that his status as Dickinson's leading citizen placed him above the law—making him "The Law" in the bayou area. The State of Texas disagreed, and Ranger Shackley gave the mayor an ultimatum, surrender or face the consequences. Bill Shackley had a reputation of being tough, but being honest—and being the fastest draw in the Texas Rangers.

Mayor Colby was also known for being tough and quick on the draw. He wasn't known for being smart, however, and the decision to draw against Shackley was, to say the least, ill-advised.

Paco and Sheriff Clayborn arrived in Dickinson moments before the shootout and kept watch for any of Mayor Colby's friends in case they wanted to backshoot the Texas Ranger. None did, so while the local doctor bound up the mayor's wound in front of the Oleander Saloon, they rode up to where Bill Shackley stood and bid him their hellos.

"Good morning, Dawes," Shackley said to the sheriff.

"Good morning, Bill. Trouble, I see?"

"Not anymore. Soon as the doc fixes that leg, I'm gonna haul our good mayor over to Austin to stand trial. The train ought to be here in about an hour."

"Need any help?"

"Nope. As usual, you're a day late and a dollar short. Say, did your wife have that baby yet?"

"Sure did, two days ago. A boy. We named him Sam after my father."

"Well, congratulations. That calls for a drink. Who's your friend?"

"This here is Paco Lopez. Best dang tracker you ever saw. He's good with a gun, too, if you ever need someone on the trail."

"Morning, Paco. *Cómo estás?*"

"*Hola,* Ranger. *Muy bien, gracias.*"

"Where'd you meet up with him?" Shackly looked at the sheriff.

Clayborn laughed. "Oh, I ran across him this morning out on Mac-Cullaugh's ranch. You might say he was just *hanging* around out there."

Shackly raised an eyebrow sensing there was a story to be told but didn't question the two men any further.

All three stepped inside the Oleander and found a table in a quiet corner of the saloon. After ordering their drinks, Sheriff Clayborn asked Paco for details on what happened at the MacCullaugh ranch.

"You know that half-witted goat I got... the one that runs away all the time? I was looking for him and strayed over on MacCullaugh's land. They got no fences out there. I didn't find Ol' *Estupido,* but I see one of MacCullaugh's calves trapped in a bog without its momma."

Paco took a long swallow of his beer and sat the glass down on the rough-wood table. He wiped his mouth with the back of his hand.

"I see tracks where the momma cow went into the bog and never came out. Arley Wade and his boys rode up as I was pulling the calf out of the bog. They say I am stealing Mister MacCullaugh's calf and they gonna string me up."

"I saw them do that," Clayborn chimed in. "Didn't seem right to me. Like so many Anglos, they don't need excuses to hang a Mexican. But you're not Mexican. You're Tejano. Your daddy fought at the Alamo alongside my uncle and all the other defenders."

"*Si, amigo.* My pappa was *Mestizo*—mixed race—Indian and pure Spanish, and my mother was pure Spanish descent, but she was from Coahuila de Zaragoza, so to men like MacCullaugh, my skin is brown. That makes me different. To him, I am Mexican."

"You're a Texan. Plain and simple."

"I agree," Ranger Shackley said. He set his empty glass on the table and stood up. "You fellas take it easy. I got some tracking to do after I drop the mayor off in Austin. Got some horse thieves running a herd of mustangs toward the rail yards in Dallas. And, Dawes, MacCullaugh ain't the man you need to watch out for. You made an enemy by shaming Arley Wade in front of his men. You watch your back, *hombre.*"

Clayborn laughed, but the look in his eyes showed a hardness that said he already knew what could happen. In his mind, he had already figured he and Wade would someday tie up. They'd had run-ins in the past. Someday, he would have to kill Arley Wade or go down from one of Wade's bullets.

"That I will, my friend." He reached up and shook Bill Shackley's hand. "Say, if you're tracking someone you ought to take Paco with you. He's got eyes like an eagle. Besides, he needs to stay out of sight for a day or two just in case that wild bunch comes looking for him."

"How 'bout it, Paco? Want to get out of town for a while?"

"*Si*, Ranger. I ride with you. You gonna pay me?"

Bill Shackly laughed. "Sure, two-bits a day."

"What about your goat?" Clayborn asked.

"Aw, he come home when he get hungry. Or I buy another goat now I got money coming to me."

All three men laughed, and Clayborn stayed behind for another beer while the Ranger and Paco took off to be fitted for the trail.

Sheriff Clayborn drained the last swallow from his glass and rose to leave.

Ever mindful of the Ranger's warning, he stopped short of the bat wing doors of the saloon and glanced up and down the street. Not seeing any trouble, he swung open one side of the doors and stepped out onto the wooden sidewalk.

The town seemed quiet enough. Kids played chase in the dusty yards. A few horses stayed hitched outside stores and the other cantinas up and down the main street. Across from the Oleander, a Mexican sat braced against a wall, strumming a guitar. His head bent over under the large *sombrero* he wore. The sheriff could hear him mumble a few lines to a popular song in English, "El Corrido de Kiansas."

Life that day in Dickenson, Texas, under a hot sun looked like any other lazy afternoon. Just then, a dynamite blast ripped through the air and blue-gray smoke spilled out of the front door of Waymore's Bank two blocks down the street.

Sheriff Clayborn drew his six-shooter and took off in a run toward the bank.

"I knew I should have hit the trail with Paco and the ranger," he said.

Reaching the corner of the bank building, Sheriff Clayborn had an inspiration. He ducked behind the building where he encountered four men mounting their horses. Each had a sack of money they'd stolen from the bank, and each one pulled up on their reins when they saw the sheriff. One of them was Arley Wade.

"Hold it right there. You're all under arrest."

"When pigs can fly," Wade shouted and pulled his gun.

Shots rang out and bullets flew wildly between the two men. Others near Wade jerked on their reins and scooted out of the line of fire. Miraculously, no one got hit. That included Sheriff Clayborn and Wade himself. Wade pulled the trigger one more time and the resounding click as the hammer fell on a spent cartridge ran through the outlaw like a lightning bolt gone wild.

"You're done, Wade. You men, drop your weapons and dismount."

By that time, a handful of citizens had armed themselves and rushed behind the bank to give the sheriff a hand. All four men followed Sheriff Clayborn's orders and lined up in a single file to be escorted to jail. When the cell door closed, Wade grinned at the sheriff.

"I guess you got the better of me this time, Sheriff. Can't for the life of me understand how we both missed each other, though, close as we were to each other."

"You never know what's going to happen in a gunfight, Wade. I'm glad I didn't hit you. I'll be even gladder to see the look on your face when the judge sentences you to prison."

"You better hope it's a long sentence, Sheriff. That'll give you years to think about what it's gonna be like when I get out. I'll see you again."

"I'll look forward to it." Sheriff Clayborn turned the key in the lock and walked out of the cellblock. Just another day of fighting crime in a dusty Texas town.

—Arkansas Hall of Fame writer Del Garrett's first attempt at writing fiction, a Civil War short story, was published in 1975 by Louis L'Amour Western Magazine. *His first book won an international award for Best Historical Western Fiction. He has also been published in* Pro Se Productions, Blood Moon Rising, Gateway Science Fiction, *and* Storyteller Magazine. *He attended workshops and mentored under prolific western author Dusty Richards. But his writing didn't stop there. He is the author of seven novels:* Lollapalooza Stories Cajun Style, Texas Justice, While the Angels Slept, Shadowlight, The Buccaneer's Daughter, The El Dorado Trail, *and* Whispers in the Wind—The Search for Jack the Ripper, *plus a crime novella series featuring 1940's private detective Felix Nash, and an anthology of short stories he calls* Del Garrett's Flea Market Tales. *Del graduated from journalism school in Indianapolis, Ind., in 1979, and took post-graduate courses in Communication Theory and Practice at Oklahoma University in 1981. His career as a journalist spanned 30 years working on newspapers, magazines and in radio and television. An award-winning poet, his poetry has been published by the Missouri State Poetry Society.*

Gaucho Oriental by Herman W. Hansen

GOING, GOING, GONE

JAMES A. TWEEDIE

THIS STORY MEANDERS its way from Nebraska to Silver City and the lost Adams diggings in New Mexico, but it's mostly a story about Pa and me and how it all played out.

When Ma died of the fever in May of 1872, Pa decided he'd had enough of homesteading in Nebraska. On the day she was buried, while we were standing beside the grave, he said to me, "For three years, I've sweated blood trying to improve this land, and the only thing I have to show for it is a dead wife."

I was fourteen years old at the time, and soon after the funeral, Pa heard about the General Mineral Act signed by President Grant.

"Listen, Beau," he said over an evening meal of corn grits and bacon, "the president says we can go out on public land and dig up gold, silver, or whatever else tickles our fancy. I've read that in places like California, Colorado, Nevada, and near everywhere else in the west, there's lots of folks living in big, fancy mansions—all because they hit paydirt. I reckon you and I find our own mother lode before other folks find it first."

Pa got a far-away look in his eyes which—so far as I could tell—wasn't a bad thing since it was a better look than the blank stare he'd had since Ma up and died.

The thought of gold seemed to bring him back to life, and his decision to head west and claim his share of the wealth immediately became the all-consuming passion of his existence.

"It's there just waiting for us," he said dreamily, "and time's a-wasting, boy. Go pack whatever you can carry and let's get at it!"

Within days, he had traded the homestead, the cabin, the freshly-planted fields, and three miles of fencing for a hundred dollars and two horses with saddles already on their backs ready to ride.

The hundred dollars ran out before we reached Pueblo, Colorado, so the two of us spent the rest of the summer and fall moving cattle from one field to another and helping to harvest wheat, corn, and other crops that came ripe just as the frost began to creep down from the Rockies.

When the last harvest was done, Pa added up the money and announced it was time for us to start prospecting in New Mexico.

Now, everybody who knew anything knew that if there was any gold to be found in New Mexico, the Spanish had already dug it up, and that the Apaches were standing in line to take a scalp from anyone who tried poking their noses into their territory. But Pa didn't pay no mind to such gossip.

"It's there," he said. "Folks just haven't looked in the right place for it yet."

For the next two years, we travelled north, south, east, and west across New Mexico, suffering through two freezing winters and surviving two summers that were hot enough to boil water without the need for a fire.

The only tools Pa carried were two pickaxes, four small hand picks, a pan, and a shovel. Over time, he went through three of the small picks, wearing down the points to a nub by chipping away at nearly every exposed rock shelf, cliff, or boulder we hit upon.

I told him a thousand times that he was looking for something that wasn't there, and towards the beginning, he'd argue back that I was still a kid and didn't know what I was talking about.

Even so, in spite of the arguing and Pa's fruitless foolishness, we enjoyed being together. Nearly every evening, we watched the mountains turn from powder red at sunset to deep purple in the afterglow. And the stars at night seemed so much closer in the high mountains than they ever did back in Nebraska. We were having the adventure of a lifetime—an adventure that quickly hardened me into a man.

As months turned to years, I began to notice that whenever we went from one place to another, Pa's mind seemed to fall farther and farther behind until it got so far away it couldn't catch up. To put it straight, Pa's brain wore down to a nub, same as his picks.

Whether he had a sickness or whether three years fighting in the war broke something in his head, I couldn't tell. All I knew was that it got to where Pa not only stopped arguing but gave up on talking altogether.

I didn't mind the silence—at least not much. But the saddest thing— and the thing I missed the most—was when he stopped laughing. Not that he was angry or sad or anything—but simply that he had become a mere shadow of the man he'd been before, mindlessly roaming about and randomly chipping away at rocks as if he expected to find a mansion inside the next one he picked at.

Pa grew a beard and quit bathing—avoiding even the touch of water when we'd pass a river, stream, or watering hole.

"The smell keeps the Apaches away," he said without the hint of a smile.

"Not to mention everything else that breathes," I muttered under my gagging breath.

The stench would've kept me away, too, but Pa became so obsessed with looking for gold that if I hadn't taken on the job of finding food and fixing it for him, he might well have starved to death from forgetting to eat.

Since people can't spend gold when they don't have any, I had to find other ways to pay for the food and whatever else we needed to survive.

It got so bad that I was asking complete strangers on the trail if they had any food or money to spare.

One of the few places where anyone actually found gold in New Mexico was in Silver City, a town that had sprung up from nothing after the touch of King Midas was discovered nearby in 1870. Claims had been staked out in all directions, but for Pa and me it wasn't gold or silver that we needed—it was finding work so we could earn enough money to survive.

So, I pushed and pulled Pa across New Mexico, from the Sangre de Cristo Mountains, through Santa Fe, and all the way down to the southwest corner of the territory. As soon as we came to Silver City, I pushed and pulled Pa into Silva Creek.

Pa came out of the water sputtering and fuming.

"Whatcha go and do *that* for?" he screamed.

"Because you stink so bad no one will hire us!" I yelled back.

Buried somewhere deep inside my father there must have been a shred of sanity left, because when I was through explaining why I'd baptized him, he said, "Right, Son. It was good of you to think of it."

It was now 1874, and late in the year. Pa was only forty-years old but looked like he was sixty. His body was strong, but his mind was as weak as the whisky they served us in the saloon.

"What brings you to this God-forsaken place?" The question came from a man standing next to us at the bar.

He was probably the same age as Pa but looked younger. His gnarled hands, weathered face, and tangled beard were accompanied by a cheerful laugh that reminded me how much I missed it in Pa.

"Father and son?" he asked.

Pa was standing next to me looking like a man who had just realized his brain was missing and was trying to remember where he'd left it

"Pa?" I said while poking him in the ribs with my elbow.

When he didn't respond, I turned to the man and said, "Yes, sir. That's what we are. Colin and Beau Eliot. I'm the one named Beau."

"Is your father all right?" the man asked with a sincere look of concern in his face.

"Pa's a good man, and he's just fine, and thank you, sir, for asking. Now, if you'd– "

"Need work?" the man interrupted. "I could use some men with good honest hands like yours."

I looked at my hands and couldn't see where they looked any more honest than anyone else's, but at that moment, I didn't really care about my hands or who the man was or what work he had in mind.

"Whatever you're offering," I said, "as long as bed and board's a part of it, we're in."

"No bed," he said, "'cepting I'll get you a tent like mine if you need one. But if you don't mind eating what I fix for myself, it's a deal. Fifty cents a day for each of you when I've got it and ten percent of whatever we dig up."

Pa didn't know half of what was going on, but he shook hands with the man the same as I did, and that's how we came to be hooked up with Willie Broder and the five acres of dirt, sagebrush, and juniper he called his Baltic Diggings.

It was early evening when we shook hands, and by the time we followed Willie the two miles or so it took to get to Chloride Flats the sun had gone down and the air felt cold enough to snow.

It never did snow on us that winter, although there were times when the hail came down an inch deep and flattened our tents. It was cold, sure enough, but we kept warm digging through the dirt and sand, sifting and panning as we went while setting aside the gold dust and flecks of silver that had drawn Willie to the spot two years earlier.

We needed water for the panning, and there wasn't any where we were digging so Willie hired a fifteen-year-old orphan boy from town, whose mother had just died the year before, to fetch water for us. Everybody knew his name was McCarty like his Mama, but when he took on calling himself Henry Antrim we all went along with it.

It turned out that after the boy didn't show up five days out of ten, Willie turned him out.

From then on, it was just the three of us again.

On the Thirteenth of March, I found Pa standing like a statue staring at something in his hand.

"Whatcha got there, Pa?"

As usual, he didn't answer, but instead of talking, he held up a gold nugget the size of my thumbnail.

For the first time in six months, Pa smiled. As soon as he got the smile up and going, he let out a whoop loud enough to bring Willie running up from camp. When Willie saw the nugget, he started dancing a jig, and Pa and I joined in like we were back in Nebraska doing the Virginia Reel with Ma.

Pa had uncovered a small stretch of fractured bedrock shale with a small seam filled with dolomite and peppered with flecks of gold large enough to pick up with our fingers.

"Hush, now, you hear?" Willie whispered in a tone of voice that folks use when they're talking in church. "Don't tell nobody what we've found, or the claim will get jumped, and we'll be dead before the week is out. It's time for me to get on down to the courthouse and incorporate this here enterprise as the Baltic Mine!"

"Pa," I said when Willie was gone, "you finally did it. And ten per cent of that nugget and ten per cent of everything under our feet is ours! Pa! Do you hear me? Do you understand? We're rich!"

Pa didn't understand a word I said, and I knew it. But I had to say it to somebody, and in any case, Pa still knew what gold looked like, and later that night when he fell asleep, he was still smiling.

When Willie came back, he said Sheriff Whitehall told him Henry Antrim had been caught stealing food, again. "The sheriff says he's a likeable kid who's stealing because he's hungry and not because he's a criminal. He also said that if he steals again, he'll have to arrest him. I think the boy's no good. Wouldn't trust him any further than I can spit."

The boy later changed his name to William H. Bonney and, by the time he was shot dead in 1881, most folks knew him as Billy the Kid.

That summer we started digging a shaft but after twenty feet the seam disappeared and the dream of getting rich began to fade.

Pa was getting to where he'd stop working and just wander off. After this happened for the third time, and we didn't find him for several hours, Willie and I agreed Pa's working days were over.

Since someone had to look after Pa full-time, I had to quit along with him.

Folks in the adjoining camps spread gossip into town that Pa was a menace to himself and to everyone else.

"He needs to be locked up," they said.

"That boy of his ought to put him in an institution," said the folks in town, "and if he won't do it, then we'll get the judge to do it for him."

I didn't know what an "institution" was, but I knew I didn't want Pa to be put in one, so I did the only thing I could think to do—I took Pa and headed north into the high mountains where no one could take him away.

We weren't rich, like we'd hoped, but the ten percent of the gold we dug up kept clothes on our backs and bought enough food for me, Pa, and the horses to live on.

Pa's gold fever turned out to be contagious, and by the time I left Silver City, I was eighteen-years old and near desperate to dig up some gold of my own.

I'd heard stories of the Lost Adams Diggings—an exposed lode of gold found by prospectors in a narrow canyon in western New Mexico back in 1864. Apaches had killed all but two of them before they could mark the spot, and of the two that survived, one left for good and the other one, who went by the name Adams, couldn't remember the way back to the gold.

So that's why I headed north, figuring that it was better to look for something that was already there rather than to look for something that might not exist at all.

Adams had said that in order to get to where they found the gold they had to squeeze through a place in the canyon that was so narrow they had to go through one at a time.

Three weeks after leaving Silver City, I felt a sudden urge to ride up a small dry arroyo that twisted its way into a nearby hill. It was late in the day, and I figured it would offer us a safe and protected place to spend the night. Up in the arroyo, the walls narrowed to a space only a few feet wide, but by the time we got there, it was already too dark to explore any further.

I laid out our camp, built a fire, and cooked up some beans for supper while Pa sat passively with the same blank look in his eyes that he'd had after Ma died.

As I checked the horses, I noticed something lying on the dark, sandy ground.

It was a gold nugget almost the same size as the one Pa had found back at Willie's mine.

I ran my fingers through the sand and found another, almost as large as the first.

Tomorrow! I thought to myself.

"Tomorrow!" I whispered in Pa's ear.

That night, Pa slept the sleep of the dead, and I couldn't sleep at all.

Sometime after midnight, I heard the unmistakable crack of distant thunder. The sound echoed overhead and whispered its way down the arroyo.

A moment later, our camp lit up like it was mid-day, and the crack and roar of thunder arrived at the same moment that my eyes were blinded by the flash of lightning.

It began hailing, and as I jumped up to calm the horses, it began raining like I never saw it rain before or since.

"Pa!" I yelled as loudly as I could. "Wake up! We've got to get out of here."

But my warning came too late, and even if he'd heard me, it wouldn't have changed the way things turned out.

Amidst the roar of the rain and thunder, I sensed what was coming.

The ground began to vibrate and then began trembling.

As I let go of the horses and ran to get Pa, a wall of water exploded through the place where the canyon narrowed, something I could hear and imagine, but not actually see, in the dark-clouded night-time darkness.

The water quickly rose and swirled around my legs—sweeping me off my feet and throwing me against the canyon wall.

In frantic desperation, I grasped at the rock and felt my fingers slide into a deep crack.

With my other hand, I reached up and found another, pulling myself higher until I was safely above the water raging below.

"Pa!" I screamed into the darkness, knowing full well that he had been swept away and was never going to hear the sound of my voice again.

The storm quickly passed, and as the sound of thunder slowly faded into the distance, I carefully climbed down the canyon wall and stood on ground that moments earlier had been under four feet of water—water that had sped through the arroyo like a train roaring through a tunnel.

As I carefully felt my way down the canyon, I called out for Pa and listened for the sound of our horses.

With the first dim light of dawn, I found my horse, dead and broken, one hundred feet down from the mouth of the arroyo. Pa's horse stood trembling, alive and unharmed, fifty feet away.

I couldn't tell whether Pa had been drowned or broken, but when I found his body further down, half-buried in the sand, his eyes were still open with the same blank stare he had taken with him to bed the night before.

With all the love and tenderness I had in my heart, I carried him up the arroyo and passed through the canyon's narrow gate as if it were the entrance to heaven itself. Not far beyond was a wider space with a high rock shelf to one side that tempted me to climb up to see what was on top of it.

There I found a rusted pick and a leather pouch filled with gold nuggets lying next to a partially-chiseled seam of quartz—quartz surrounded by more gold than I had ever imagined possible.

I took the pouch and climbed down to where I began to dig deep into the sand that filled the arroyo floor. Each press of my spade exposed even more nuggets, which I left untouched.

When the hole was deep enough, I covered Pa's face with his bandana, lowered him into the grave, and covered him with the sand.

I didn't say a prayer, but I remembered words from Jesus that Ma had read to me when she was suffering from the fever that took her.

"'In my Father's house are many mansions... I go to prepare a place for you.'"

They say the streets of heaven are paved with gold.

With those thoughts, I left Pa behind, buried in the mansion of his dreams, and turned his horse toward Arizona, where, not long after, I met up with a prospector named Ed Schieffelin.

What came of that is another story altogether.

—James A. Tweedie has lived in California, Utah, Scotland, Australia, Hawaii, and presently in Long Beach, Washington. He has published six novels, four collections of poetry, and one collection of short stories with Dunecrest Press. His award-winning stories and poetry have appeared in regional, national, and international print and online anthologies. He is a regular contributor to Frontier Tales *and* Saddlebag Dispatches.

He recalls moving from San Francisco to Logan, Utah, in 1979 and being both baffled and amused when he was asked, "What made you decide to move out West from California?"

In that moment, he learned that "the West" was not just a direction, but a cultural space infused with traditions and tales embracing a heritage of mountain men, pioneers, Native Peoples, cowboys, homesteaders, prospectors, ranchers, railroads, and a host of conflicts that stretched and expanded the United States into the country it is today.

His favorite corner of the West is the Sierra Nevada, where he has hiked and fly fished since he was old enough to walk.

A MYTH IN THE REMAKING

KEVIN BROWN

THAT MAY, THE renowned gunslinger stepped off the Carson Stage. It was clear the reputation had overtaken the man. The young nurse had just finished her morning shift and now stood beneath the resort's porte-cochère watching the coachman unload a steamer trunk while the consumptive waited in a whiskey and laudanum stupor. His shoulders stooped him shorter than the wagon's rear wheel as he leaned on a silver-headed cane. A jeweled gambler's ring on his right pinky winked in the dim light. He was dressed like a dandy in black city boots and slouch hat, silver brocade vest and crimson cravat fastened with a diamond stickpin. The gold fob of his pocket watch festooned from a pearl button. A gray frock coat sueded with arrow yokes draped his frail frame like an ulster cape. One side flap skinned back from the frogmouth pocket of his dark trousers worn loose from the old weight of his Colt Lightning. The scenery along Eighth and Grand stood frozen in a tableau vivant of halted wagons and clustered gawkers as two bellboys from the sanitorium rushed out to the stagecoach and took up the trunk. The legend bent in a sudden coughing fit—hacking a fine red mist into an ivory silk kerchief. Recapturing his breath, he gimped past the nurse touching the curled brim of his hat.

"Madame," he said with the genteel cadence of a Byronic aristocrat, a shoulder-holstered pistol butt shaping the coat at his left flank. Then, John Henry Holliday entered the Hotel Glenwood to survive and to die in November of the year Eighteen and Eighty-seven.

NESTLED AMONG THE western flanks of the Rockies, Glenwood Springs was a small but prospering camp situated in a quiet valley near the confluence of the Colorado and Roaring Fork Rivers. Named for its sulphur springs and vapor caves, claimed by the Utes to possess curative powers, the high altitude and crisp cold also provided a hospitable climate for consumptives.

It also offered a brand-new resort—The Hotel Glenwood.

A modern three-story establishment, a combination hotel and pesthouse, consisted of seventy-five rooms and a restaurant. It boasted electricity, hot and cold running water, and private baths while providing an elevator and medical staff.

And for the duration of Doc Holliday's stay, his life, the nurse following him inside would be charged with tending his morning needs along with the first shift bellboy, George Weirick, who now escorted him to the lift. The mesh doors closed, and the infamous dentist turned gambler and gunfighter ascended. Pale and hacking, he faded from sight, then sound.

HER FIRST MORNING as Holliday's nurse began like any other, though it almost ended with a bang. She rose before dawn, dressing in a floor-length gown of black tweed, the leg-o-mutton sleeves tight to the elbow, bulbed to the shoulder, then set out for the hotel.

Consulting Doc's clipboard, she tied on an apron and shoulder bib, attached her badge and satin cape, then buckled to her cinched belt a waist clasp clipped with nursing essentials. As the late shift gossiped, she slipped on a broadcloth trimmed with passementerie gimps. Adjusted her pleated mobcap and began her rounds.

The grifter had been all night at the gambling halls so she performed her duties in stockinged feet as he slept. When an abrupt coughing fit startled her to yelp, Doc sprang upright, a nickel-plated .41 Thunderer in one hand and a .38 Lightning in the other.

"Why, Madam," he said, "we meet again." Eyes lidded, Doc spun the pistols opposite directions on trigger fingers and slid them back beneath the blanket. Another coughing spell seized him, and he hacked dark mucous laced with blood into his kerchief. He lay back, wheezing. Voice graveled from throat ulcers, he said, "If I but woke to such angelic light more often."

She returned to the lounge with a pallid countenance.

"Are you well?" asked Mr. Weirick.

"Terminal as Mister Holliday may be," she said, shuddering. "He sure wakes with stormy Colts."

LATER, MARSHAL J.W. SCOTT greeted Doc in the lobby.

"Morning, John," said Scott. "What's on our agenda this fine day?"

Doc mopped the sheen of sweat from his brow with a handkerchief then fished from his paisley waistcoat a hunter-case pocket watch. "Seems my coffers are in need of replenishment," he said, sprung the lid, checked the time. "Somewhere a tiger needs bucking."

"Feeling lucky, are we?"

Doc snapped the lid shut, slipping the fob watch back in its pocket slit. "Don't we look it?"

After a few days on Holliday's heels, Marshal Scott figured him too sick for much foolery and left him be.

Still, others needed a little longer separating the man from the myth. Curious patrons of saloons and haberdasheries, barbershops and other industries of trade filled every window, doorway, and tent flap, watching him pass along Grand. Speculating as to whether this worn figure sporting a gambler hat was a brave hero or bunco hellion, cold-blooded cut-throat, or confidence man with a death wish.

Reenacting showdowns with finger pistols, youths often froze walleyed at his presence, trying to reckon the infamous desperado from the papers involved in gunfights and vendetta rides with this gaunt degenerate in stiff collars and notched lapels. Some even approached him, spouting questions about Tombstone and the Earps, the "Cow-Boys," and the O.K. Corral.

"It was an awful thing," he'd reply, staring off in the distance but seeing back in time.

As the novelty faded, Doc got on well with most, even gaining employment as a bartender and faro dealer to support himself.

Keeping late hours, he often slept through the mornings, always leaving two dollars for Mr. Weirick—one for a handle of whiskey, the other a tip. Sometimes he'd wake to the nurse tending her chores, and, in an educated drawl made cursive by drink and drug, he'd inquire about her life. Though shy at first, with time she came to talk so much that, by shift's end, her voice was hoarse as his.

She knew nothing of Doc's past save overheard hearsay, nor did she care about any fame or infamy associated with his name. The man in her ward possessed a mannered and genial disposition, and she'd taken to his welcome company.

Once, she arrived to find him spiffed up awaiting her accompaniment to August W. Dennis's photography studio, a makeshift tent near the river, for what would become the last photo of John Henry Holliday.

As Doc's time in Glenwood passed, he received visits from neither kith nor kin, despite later inventive claims. And, most correspondence the nurse handled on his behalf was with his first cousin, Martha Ann "Mattie" Holliday, also known as Sister Mary Melanie. In mere months, she'd be the lone relative listed in Holliday's obituary. Forty-nine years later, the nurse would learn Doc's beloved Mattie had become a legend herself, serving as inspiration for Melanie Hamilton in Margaret Mitchell's *Gone with the Wind*.

ONE EVENING, THE nurse walked into The Mirror Saloon. Eyes watched her from the faro banks in back. She stood at the bar where Doc appeared almost incandescent in the smoky light.

"Why, Madam," he said, sleeve cuffs turned back to the elbows. "What occasion brings a peach to such iniquitous...." His voice dragged into a coughing bout, and he stifled it with his neckerchief. He cleared his throat and smiled.

"Can't a hardworking citizen relax in her down time?"

"Indeed." He winked. "But she shan't pay on my watch." Selecting a bottle of Old Overholt Rye, he watched in the back bar mirror Charlie "Big Bear" Daughton rise and stalk toward her—trailing an air of ill-intent and ill-odor.

"Boys," Daughton said, "we got us a soiled dove done flew in." He bellied to the bar and leaned on an elbow, a plug of chaw knotting his jaw. Flashing a pumpkin smile of black teeth, he said, "The Pat Carr harlotry hovel's on Riverfront."

"Daughton, can't you differentiate between a guardian angel and a painted cat?" Doc poured her a shot. "Aphroditic Saint," he said, gesturing toward her. "Now, Charlie, just picture your mother."

Laughter shot Daughton upright. He malleted a fist on the scarred bar-top and sneered back, silencing it.

"I just stopped to check on John," the nurse said. "Uh, I mean—Mister Holliday."

Daughton spat over a spittoon, amber tobacco juice slashing the sawdust floor, and snorted at his pals. "Think ol' Doc's got himself a parri-*mour.*"

"Teddy Bear," Doc said. "Your frustrations of the flesh seep through its filth."

Laughter again. Daughton reached inside his jacket, but Doc seized his arm. "Keep your sick mitts off me," Big Bear said, snatching free.

"I'll go," the nurse said, but the ruffian grabbed her.

"Charlie Daughton!" Doc hollered, his voice hard. And though pale as enameled porcelain, a bib of sweat darkening his pastel shirt, he somehow appeared strong. Almost healthy. Dangerous. "Maybe I'll just plug you where you stand wasting space."

"For an unheeled lunger," he said, letting go, "that jaw sure wobbles."

Doc grinned. "Sings too."

Daughton stared, a scar slashing one socket where a dead eye lazed toward the nurse backing away. She clipped a table, and he jarred, pulling at her, but Doc had already skinned a Derringer from the small of his back. Both barrels near point-blank at the longrider's face. He tongued the wad in his jaw, glancing down to find the gunslinger had somehow also drawn a Colt revolver, whistling his ease with it pointed at Big Bear's belly.

Doc nodded and the nurse slipped out the batwing doors. "I propose we remain practical in our predicament."

Someone hollered, "Learn him, Doc!"

"Shut up, Hyman," Daughton said without looking. "Holliday, what you flannel-mouthing about?"

"What say you return to your table—get back on the win," he said. "Preserve your sand in front of your friends."

"And if I don't?"

"Then by all means let your irons bark," Doc said with a Cheshire cat smile. "And die in front of them."

They stood in this dime western showdown— a silent tableau, save Doc's cheek pulsing with choked coughs. His Adam's Apple worked to stem them.

Daughton weighed his options with a drooped idiot's lip and darting eye then grinned, lassoed a finger aloft. "Bug Juice, all around!"

Doc tipped his head in an element of *noblesse oblige*. Then just as fast as they'd appeared, his instruments of death were gone.

It was the last time he'd ever draw them.

ADDED TO DOC'S consumption was his heavy indulgence in alcohol and opium which began affecting his capacity to work along with his mental faculties at the card tables. He also began to suspect the vaporous springs he'd hoped would ease his ailments were somehow exacerbating them.

By summer's end, John's body was ravaged. His pallor sallow with sunken eyes peering from a skeletal face like a child in a spook mask. His heart rate was erratic. He developed the consumptive's unmistakable "graveyard cough" and began suffering hemorrhages from his mouth and nose. He'd watched the same disease take his mother and adoptive brother, so Doc knew he'd reached the terminal stage.

Soon, the dignity with which he conducted himself faded. He'd cough several wild rags bloody every day and often soiled himself with violent diarrhea. The nurse cleaned his slops and washed his linens. She prepared his untouched meals and changed his unmentionables. Bathing him one morning, she found leprous sores pocking his body. John had at last reached "Galloping Consumption."

The days following, Doc turned to religion, having acquaintances with a Catholic priest and Presbyterian minister. Well-versed in theology, he may've been seeking a spiritual peace in the afterlife he never found in this one.

Sick as he'd become, Doc was still a barkeep when fall began. His faded clothes now worn threadbare. He eased through town brittle of body and spirit. Evident by his downcast gaze, his cane and bootheels clopping out an aching gait.

In September, pneumonia again forced him to bed where he'd only rise twice more.

----◄●►----

AS THE MONTH passed, Glenwood Springs began preparations for the upcoming arrival of the Denver & Rio Grande Railroad. The rutted streets thrummed with anticipation, but for Doc, the celebration would bring the railroad's surgeon, Dr. W. W. Crook.

It wouldn't matter.

By the time the doctor reached Glenwood on October fifth, Doc's end was fast approaching. Under Crook's supervision, he remained bedridden, listening to the parades and fireworks and banquets outside.

One morning, Holliday lay sleeping, his face corpselike, the pillow propping his head soaked through with sweat.

The nurse had gotten him clean with fresh bedding and was about to tote the laundry down when she heard his opiated chuckle.

"What's got you so tickled?" she asked, tracing his deadpan gaze to his bare toes wriggling from the blanket. Then, he drew a drowned breath as his eyes rolled white and fluttered closed.

Detecting at his neck a faint blood beat, she rushed for the doctor. Over the next two weeks, he'd slip in and out of a coma. Waking in an almost lucid delirium, then drifting off again.

When the nurse arrived on November eighth, the overnight staff informed her Doc was awake but that he hadn't spoken in almost twenty-four hours.

At first sight, he appeared dead, so pale and emaciated was he, lying still, save the faint spasms of tussis beneath the cover. His eyes vacant, perhaps lost in the replayed unfurling of his short life. He didn't speak when she changed his bed linens, nor as she sponged him clean. But while she prepared breakfast, he whispered. "Madam?"

"Yes, John."

He licked his cracked lips. "May I trouble you for a courtesy?"

"Why, you're no trouble at all."

He worked his eyes toward her. "A taste of whiskey?"

She crooked her mouth. "Promise you won't tell the doctor?"

"On my life," he mumbled, a hint of a smile. "I'll take it to my grave."

She opened the carafe of Old Overholt and brimmed his ornate silver cup. Placing it in his slender hands, she slid a chair bedside.

"From the bugs to the worms," he said with a feeble toast. His trembling hand sloshing the whiskey. He sipped, licked his ashen mustache, and whispered, *"Animam agere."*

He nipped the cup dry—savoring each taste as if it were his first, his last. A single tear pearled an eye, and he began to chuckle, again wriggling his toes from the blanket.

Then they stilled. And his chuckle fell silent.

She looked back.

His lips had parted with his slackened jaw. The tear running the hollow of his cheek as his livid eyes stared but saw no more.

She sat several minutes in silence, watching a few flakes of early snow skelter past the window from a blanched November firmament. Then she asked Mr. Weirick to call on Dr. Crook and returned to the room. She sat bedside, waiting.

Soon, the physician arrived with the bellboy. Pressed fingertips to Doc's wrist, then worked the wrapping from his neck for his carotid. "Fetch the mortician," he said, and Weirick stepped out.

Dr. Crook looked the dead man over. Not much more than a skull stretched with translucent skin. His feet still jutted from the blanket. He passed a hand over Doc's eyes, closing them. Drew the bedsheet over his head, opened a little notebook, and with a pencil nub wrote—

10:00 a.m. Tuesday. November 8, 1887. John Henry "Doc" Holliday, 36 years of age. Chronic Pulmonary Tuberculosis (Consumption).

He paused to inquire about Doc's last minutes.

The nurse studied the shape of the man who'd go down as one of the most infamous figures from this fabled time. Through the years, the creation of the "Holliday Mystique" would raise him ten feet tall and killing upwards of thirty men.

"He requested a tumbler of rye," she said, "which I obliged."

Crook jotted in his notebook.

The nurse eased the sheet up and took Doc's cold hand. A hand that'd be called one of the quickest and deadliest ever with a six-shooter. But she'd witnessed his aura firsthand in The Mirror Saloon. Knew it wasn't so much his draw, but the decision to draw that made him so dangerous.

The fear his name conjured did the rest.

She told the doctor he'd been at peace, staring down at his bare feet. "Wiggling his toes and giggling."

As with most romanticized icons, the sensational would always headline, and the major players remembered—the Cowboys and Law-men, Earps and Clantons, Wyatt, Curly Bill, Virgil, Johnny Ringo. A few lesser knowns would sometimes get mentioned in their dealings with Doc during his lifetime—people like Dr. Crook and the bellboys of the Hotel Glenwood.

The nurse, however, would be forgotten in the pages of history. Lost to the celluloid of lore.

The doctor tapped his pencil. "Giggling."

"Like before the coma," she said, blinking a sting from her eyes. "Seems he was still rather amused."

As the years passed, she'd keep up with the revisionist documentation that grew around the legend. But rare was the occasion it ever resembled the John she knew for six fleeting months in 1887. The southern gentleman who'd protect a lady from a scalawag in a saloon. The educated aristocrat who'd rather listen to another's tales than tell his own.

"Amused?" said Crook, scribbling. "Amused at what?"

Until her death in 1957, what always piqued the nurse's interest was the ever-changing speculation on Doc Holliday's final moments. Wiggling his toes, he no doubt found it funny he would die with his boots off rather than in the violent wilds of the Old West. Yet, if so, his last breath was not given to its proclamation, but to the simple laughter such irony provided.

Then the breath and the laughter ran out.

"All of it," she said. "From *Once Upon a Time* to *The End*."

<hr />

—*Kevin Brown has had two collections of short stories published by small presses:* Ink on Wood *(Virgogray Press) and* Death Roll *(Lame Goat Press). He has had fiction, poetry, and nonfiction published in over 200 literary journals, Magazines, and anthologies. He won numerous writing competitions, fellowships, and grants, including an Arkansas Governor Award and Walton Fellowship, and was also nominated for three Pushcart Prizes and two The Best American Short Stories Awards. He co-wrote the film* Living Dark, *which won a Moondance Film Festival Award and was sold to New Films International and collaborated on a television pilot with Linda Bloodworth, creator of the hit show* Designing Women. *He has been fortunate to learn under great mentors, including William Harrison (*Rollerball, *1975), Ellen Gilchrist (1984 National Book Award,* Victory Over Japan*), Molly Giles (Pulitzer Prize Nominee,* Rough Translations*), and before his passing, William Gay (*I Hate to See That Evening Sun Go Down*).*

With the Eye of the Mind by Frederic Remington

THE
PROSPEROUS PENNY

LEE CLINTON

WHEN NATHANAEL PENNY found out his wife had been messing around with one of the hands from the Pickford Ranch, he had a mind to kill them both. To build up the necessary courage to murder two people in cold blood, Nate, as he was known to all, turned to the bottle, which just brought on a bad case of melancholy. Ambition had run slap bang into reality as Nate was no gunman. Sure, he wore a gun, everybody did, but I doubt if it had left the holster in a month of Sundays. He was a cowpoke without the need or desire to learn the intricacies of gunplay, and besides, he didn't have the temperament for it. He was an ordinary man, with an ordinary disposition, living an ordinary life. Some said it was why Minnie, his wife, had strayed in the first place. She wanted more than ordinary and went looking.

At the bottom of a deep, dark well of despair and near full of liquor, Nate decided it was best to just end it all there and then. Without further thought, he pulled out his handgun, a ten-year-old Remington single action, and put the end of the barrel in his mouth. The cold metallic taste against the tongue did not deter him. He had made up his mind. He gripped and steadied the barrel with his left hand as his right thumb pulled back on the hammer rotating the cylinder to a loaded chamber while his index finger searched for the trigger. All was ready. He paused for a moment as if to bid farewell to the world around him, which was little more than a bare upstairs room in a rundown boarding house behind the stockyards on Slaughter Street, shut his eyes, and pulled the trigger. The hammer with its fixed firing pin flicked forward to strike the percussion cap at the base of the .45 cartridge.

Nothing happened.

Nate's eyes remained tightly closed, and it took him a good ten seconds before he peeked out to wonder if what he was experiencing was the afterlife. It wasn't, and he'd peed his pants just a little.

Not dissuaded from this folly, Nate started over again, pulling back on the hammer a second time to rotate the cylinder to the next bullet. Closed his eyes tight and jerked the trigger. Once again, the mechanics didn't falter, and the hammer released with a click just as it was meant to do.

Still, nothing happened.

Nate was perplexed as he sat on the side of his small iron cot. On two deliberate occasions, he had executed the ritual of suicide and failed. He took the gun from his mouth, casually pointed the barrel in the air, drew back on the hammer, and squeezed the trigger.

The sound from the shot within the confines of that small room was much like putting your head in a metal bucket as it was hit with the back of an axe handle. Nate's ears rang while the kick from the shot dislodged the pistol from his loose grip to hit the floor with a heavy clunk. The bullet, now well on its journey towards the heavens, had punched a neat hole in the pressed tin ceiling above his head and exited through the shingles on the roof.

A commotion within the boarding house followed on that late Sunday afternoon. Fellow occupants ran to Nate's room. The first to arrive was the owner, Mrs. Rose Blenkhorn, a woman of little humour who was more concerned about her ceiling than the wellbeing of her boarder. It was Jimmy Tout from across the hall who twigged as to what might have happened and enquired, "You okay, Nate?"

"Yeah, I think so," came the dazed reply.

"How so?" asked Billy Rowell, who was also a cowpoke like Nate and had been in the washroom down the hall looking at a deck of playing cards with risqué pictures of French gals taking their toilette.

"I've been sent a sign," replied a stunned Nate quietly. "No, two signs," he said a little louder. "I believe I have been saved by the Almighty Father himself."

Mrs. Blenkhorn would have none of it. "You've been drinking and fooling around with your gun, and you've shot a hole in my ceiling. Who's going to pay for that?"

The young kitchen hand, Elsie Heppel, arrived last but in time to hear the declaration of salvation and the name of the Almighty. Without thought, she said, "Praise be to God that our brother Nate has been saved. May he stay saved for all time."

This acclamation connected with Nate who agreed by saying, "Sister Elsie, you are right. I need to stay saved. I need to do the Almighty's work in praise of my deliverance."

I was called in a little later by Rose Blenkhorn to examine the hole in her ceiling. She was in a mood and out to extract the cost of repairs from Nate who didn't have but two cents to rub together. I was more concerned with law and order and asked for his pistol, which he willingly surrendered, saying that he had no need for it anymore as the Good Lord himself was looking after him personally. I said I'd give it back later, once things had settled down, and provided he wasn't going to shoot any more holes in Rose Blenkhorn's ceiling.

I took the Remington back to the office and went to unload it prior to securing the pistol in the gun cabinet. It turned out to be no easy job. Inspection of the chambers showed that one cylinder was empty, a common practice to allow the hammer to rest forward and prevent an accidental strike of the firing pin against a loaded cartridge. But boy, did I have a devil of a time in trying to extract the spent cartridge and those other four rounds of ammunition. It was as if they had been glued in place.

In seeking a solution, I asked Deputy Larry Wheeler if he had ever seen anything like it, and he said he had from a revolver found on the body of a miner out near Miles Crossing. The weapon had laid untouched and exposed to the elements for the best part of three months over a wet winter, resulting in moisture and grit getting into the cylinder to wedge each cartridge case tight in its chamber. This turned out to be the same situation with brute force being required to remove each cartridge. On close examination under a magnifying glass, it could be seen where the grit and moisture had scored and corroded each cartridge case as well as pitting the cylinder bores. Two of the rounds had the solid imprint of the firing pin upon the caps as did the spent cartridge. The percussion caps on the other two unfired rounds were untouched.

Meanwhile, Nate remained in a suspended state of sanctity. He had become more convinced than ever that he had been saved for a special purpose–whatever that was. Elsie invited him to her church that following Sunday, and with just a little prompting, she got him to tell how a dark shadow had fallen upon him and how in desperation he had considered to end it all. The congregation with eyes wide, fell silent, and leaned forward to listen. Nate looked back and blinked. Never had he been afforded such undivided attention in his life, and it gave him a confidence that seemed to lift him above his fellow parishioners.

In a strong voice, he said, "I chose the coward's way out. I chose to kill myself." The crowd gasped as one. "But on deliberately pulling the trigger, I was spared. The gun did not fire." More gasps. "Yet, in my sorry state I did it again and still that gun did not fire." Women began to fan themselves to retain composure. "I had to ask myself why," said Nate. "Was the Almighty playing with me? Was he toying like a cat playing with a wounded mouse?' The congregation was on the edge of their pews. "So, I tested the Good Lord. Yes, I did, brothers and sisters. I raised that gun toward the heavens to seek a sign and squeezed that trigger, and guess what? It fired as good as gold, and that was when I knew that I had been sanctified. I was not being taken because I had work to do here, right now, today, and tomorrow. And that's what I'm going to do. I'm here to tell you not to despair in your hour of need because God Almighty is not ready for you yet."

Every man, woman, and child leapt to their feet as one to exclaim hallelujah and swarmed forward to Nate, pressing silver coins into his palms while begging for his blessing. Not knowing exactly what he should say, he offered the words, "May you be blessed with prosperity in your earthly life." It was a good line for a spur-of-the-moment thought from a man who had spent so little time inside a church.

That following season of '85 was one of the best on record for the district. The climate was mild but with good rains and sunny days to grow the wheat and corn high. The yields were unsurpassed while the pastures were lush across the surrounding plains. Those steers were as fat as hogs and the quality of the produce was reflected in the market prices which saw all in the community flourish. The churches filled with thankful folk who wished to praise the Lord and listen to Nate as they were convinced that his blessing had brought them this prosperity. The season after that was also good, and somehow he acquired the title of Prosperous Nate Penny. That was then shortened to just Prosperous Penny by Elsie, who was now getting very good at promoting Nate in a carnival sort of way to all regardless of their denomination or faith.

Now, not everybody was convinced of Nate's ability to bestow blessed gifts from the Almighty, and as sheriff, I was paid to be sceptical about everything and anything. Doc Ferguson had a similar view and casually said to me, "Have you seen Nate Penny lately?"

I replied, "No, why?"

"He was down at the bank. Arrived in a smart buggy with Elsie Heppel. Both were gussied up. She doesn't work in the kitchen at the Indiana anymore. Her time is spent in assisting Nate with his church meetings. She is quite the businesswoman now." It was said with a touch of curious admiration. "They have a travelling road show and use a tent. Big tent. Can hold over one hundred. Even employ three boys to erect and pull it down for them."

"Good for Nate," I said without showing too much enthusiasm.

"Good! Sure is good. They pass the plate at these meetings, and talk has it they are worth a fortune from the takings."

I didn't believe it and said so.

"Then you better talk to Carl down at the bank when you next see him. He as good as confirmed that they are making the same profits out of their district prayer meetings as Pickford's is making from cattle sales."

"Really?" I questioned with more than a little astonishment.

A couple of days later, when in the office and talking about law matters, I casually asked my deputy about Nate and queried if he had attended one of his congregations. Larry said he had. In fact, everyone he knew had, so he went along to see what all the fuss was about.

"Impressed?" I asked.

"Well, it's not the Nate Penny you and I once knew. He sure knows how to spin a yarn."

"Any particular yarn?"

"The one about the two misfires. Only he doesn't call them that. It's the story that grabs the most attention, and he keeps it for last just before the plate is passed." Larry then said under his breath, "Sure is a lot of bull, if you ask me."

I wanted to know more. "How, exactly?"

Larry was a little reluctant to say and went to the door of the office and closed it. "I've learnt to be careful about what I say, in case it is seen as disparaging. My own family pulled me up on my attitude when I alluded to the two misfires just being bad-good luck."

"What's bad-good luck?" I'd never heard the saying before.

Larry leaned in close. "How many misfires have you had with ammunition over the past five years?"

Honestly, I couldn't recall one and said so.

"Me neither," said my deputy, "but we follow the rules and keep each round clean and dry, and we shoot our ammunition within the year and buy new in sealed boxes. But, if you treat them with neglect year after year, they can and will fault."

I knew this to be true and nodded in agreement.

Larry's face was serious, and I could tell that he had given this subject some serious thought. "By not keeping each cartridge dry, over time, the powder becomes susceptible to moisture. You remember that gun I told you about? The one belonging to the miner. When I was finally able to get the rounds out of each chamber, I tried firing them, and they all failed."

"So?" I said, prompting Larry to tell me more.

"So, I took each round apart. The caps had all fired correctly but failed to ignite the powder."

"Interesting," I said.

"I tried to burn the powder with a match head, and I couldn't get it to flare."

"And the bad-good luck?" I asked.

"Bad luck for you and me if we have a misfire when upholding the law."

"And the good luck?"

"Good luck if you are trying to blow your brains out with neglected ammunition while drunk as a skunk."

I couldn't help but smile. Larry had an eloquent way of summing up a situation with acute accuracy.

"I'm surprised that Nate actually got one round to fire," said Larry.

"Are you saying that Nate's two remaining rounds would have also misfired?" I asked.

"I am."

"Would you put money on it?" I said with a grin.

Larry thought for a moment. "Yes, I would."

"No need for that," I said, "but why not put it to the test. We can't do it with Nate's pistol, I gave it back, but the empty case, the two misfires and the other two unfired rounds are right here in my desk drawer."

"It's not the pistol," said Larry. "It's the ammunition."

We walked out back toward a makeshift range where we tested our weapons and Larry loaded his pistol with Nate's two unfired rounds, and without fanfare, cocked and pulled the trigger twice. Nothing happened. He was right. Both failed to fire.

When strolling back to the office, I ventured to say, "So where does that leave young Nate?"

"Apart from being alive?" quipped Larry.

"Yes," I said, "apart from that."

"Just another fraud," said Larry, "only he doesn't know it."

"A lucky fraud if the rumours of his new wealth are correct."

"It won't last," said Larry. "The only things that last in this world come from hard, honest work."

It was a perceptive comment, but then again, Deputy Sheriff Larry Wheeler was one of the most perceptive men that I would ever meet.

There are no guarantees in life and especially for those who work the land. The following season was not so kind, and the next after that was downright harsh. Most had tucked away some of the bounty from those two good seasons and managed okay. However, some did not and that included Nate and Elsie. They had come from poorly ways into unexpected wealth and somehow believed that it would last forever. This led them to be frivolous with their newfound fortune. They lived high and spent on a whim, trusting that the Almighty would never allow them to want again. The final straw came with a visit from the Bureau of Internal Revenue as Nate and Elsie had failed to declare their earnings and pay any proper amount of tax. They appealed but were judged to be running a travelling road show for the purposes of profit while not affiliated to any church or religion. Now, close to being bankrupt and facing prosecution, Elsie came up with an idea. She proposed that they re-enact Nate's deliverance by the Almighty, arguing that as it would once again astonish the congregation into gifts of generosity.

Nate was unsure.

Elsie pressed her case. It would be a repetition of his first telling of the story when he was overwhelmed with the benevolence of the parishioners. It would amaze, but this time the abundance would come from a congregation twenty-fold in size, putting an end to their financial predicament.

Nate was still hesitant.

"The Lord helps those who help themselves," was Elsie's final pitch.

Their situation was dire, reflected Nate, so reluctantly, he agreed.

"Leave it to me," said Elsie leaping into action, then adding, "and the Lord," before affectionately kissing her betrothed upon the cheek.

A temporary stage was built on the lower field just south of town at the end of Main Street, and the talents of a prominent painter of signage and stage scenery was commissioned to provide a backdrop depicting the room in Rose Blenkhorn's boarding house. Posters publicized the event in advance, which attracted a giant open-air crowd said to be a thousand or more strong who passed under a giant banner proclaiming the words The Prosperous Penny. The papers even reported that Buffalo Bill Cody would have trouble drawing a bigger crowd.

Nate proposed to use his old revolver in this public stunt, but this time Elsie took it upon herself to provide the cartridges. Brand new ones from the general store that came in a sealed cardboard box—to emerge bright, shiny, clean, and dry. As Nate was now busy preparing for his speech, she even loaded the bullets for him into his gun.

All was set and Nate came on stage twenty minutes into the proceedings dressed in white. Another idea by Elsie to ensure that he was clearly identified as the center of attention. He stood in silent wonder as he listened to a sweet rendition by the congregation of the hymn "Pass Me Not, O Gentle Savior" before stepping up into the makeshift pulpit to rousing applause. With arms outstretched, he proceeded to give a heartfelt sermon on the ways of the Lord and the need for constant faith.

All were mesmerized.

On descending from the pulpit, he walked to center stage. A small iron cot had been positioned close to the front so all could see. Sitting, to perch upon the edge, he looked up as Elsie came on stage and silently presented Nate with his gun from black gloved hands.

The crowd hushed as one.

Who on that sunny afternoon in July 1889, would forget this event even if they lived to be one hundred and one? Especially the children, dressed in Sunday-best and seated to the very front. How could their little eyes and ears forget what unfolded when Prosperous Nathanael Penny placed the barrel of his gun in his mouth and pulled the trigger.

—*The author is an Australian writer of ten Western novels published under the pen name of Lee Clinton as part of the Black Horse Western (BHW) series. Unfortunately, that line of books has now been discontinued by the publisher. However, titles such as* Raking Hell, The Mexican, Coyote, *and* Animal Instinct *remain available worldwide in digital form via Amazon. In the meantime, he has now turned his hand to short stories as he continues his love of the American Western.*

FIRST FLAKE

LISA H. OWENS

THE SKY IS beautiful tonight. Billions of stars shine down on the South Fork of the American River, and fingers of moonbeams unfurl to caress the mossy crevices beneath its rocky banks. It is a rare treat to feel the vastness of the universe and to know I exist—one tiny speck tucked away in a secluded place. I am so weary having been in a state of wakefulness for longer than I care to remember. I watch the sky from beneath a lens of crystal water. Time passes with sunshine and rain and too many cycles of the moon's phases to count, until one summer night, the coyotes in the hills sing me a lullaby and I sleep.

"CAREFUL, DUMB FOOZLER," the authoritative voice shouted to be heard above the raucous din of the construction crew. Every hammer stopped mid-stroke, and an uncomfortable silence fell over the group of skilled carpenters and Nisenan slave laborers. All eyes looked up towards Billy Hartford, the budding carpenter, teetering on a rooftop stretch of unstable scaffolding. His hammer flailing in an ungainly attempt to right himself.

"Steady there, son."

No one dared utter a sound as Captain John Sutter, a forty-five-year-old Swiss pioneer and self-bestowed captain, steadied the boy in the same manner he calmed Helvetia, his high-strung stallion when he became unhinged. He spoke in a soothing voice, and Billy visually relaxed. Everything slowed down. The flapping of his arms ceased—instead opening wide for balance like a tightrope walker's pole. The weight of the hammer in his right hand threw him off, and he struggled to adjust. Just when it looked like Billy was done-for—soon to meet his maker—he dropped the hammer and found his footing, and the work crew breathed a collective sigh of relief. Poised tools of the trade were once again set in motion.

"Hartford's oldest boy... still wet behind the ears," James Marshall, Sutter's business partner and the construction supervisor, explained away the boy's near-catastrophe as he walked Captain Sutter through the finer points of the ongoing project nearing completion after just over one year.

They trekked along the bank of the South Fork to inspect the most important element of Project Sawmill—the wooden hurdy-gurdy. Upon reaching the serene spot on the river where the Arroyo Willows flourished, Sutter stopped cold in his tracks. From this shady vantage point, it was a glorious sight to behold, this unwieldy structure that would harness the energy of water to rotate the wide wheel situated beneath the wheelhouse.

"Mein Gott, James. Never in my wildest dreams...." his words trailed off as he pulled a silk handkerchief from his pocket to covertly dab at tears threatening to spill from his deep-set eyes. He gave his nose a good honk and spat a wad of yellow phlegm into the river, watching as a current carried it downstream into the realm of the wheel where it disappeared beneath the jetty.

"Holy scheisse! The wheel spins."

He laughed and shoved the soiled hanky back into his pants pocket as the duo walked downstream and climbed the short rickety ladder leading to the main platform of the unfinished wheelhouse. Sutter scampered up and into the open-air structure with a speed that belied his age, and Marshall followed close behind. The interior of the mill was unorganized for the most part. The floor, constructed of hand-adzed boards, was a minefield of debris. They gingerly navigated around discarded nail-pegs and shards of splintered wood that peppered the floor's nooks and crannies. Small crates of equipment, scattered willy-nilly, lacked any semblance of order while in contrast the crudely squared-off logs that would fill in the one solid wall, a buffer against the north wind, were stacked with precision.

"Before the first frost...." Marshall's words trailed off when he squatted to yank a sharp splinter of wood from the sole of his left boot—well-worn and caked with a layer of horseshit.

"What a damn pig sty," he interjected, sucking air through the gap where a tooth should be.

"This pile of horseshit..." he stood and his eyes swept across the room in a critical state of disarray before he pointed down to the stinking muck on his left boot for emphasis, "will be put to order, and we'll be milling trees faster than those damn savages can chop 'em down. Mark my words."

Project Sawmill was the most recent in a series of Sutter's transformation plans. He had started building his empire with a donated set of second-hand tools and a bare-bones crew of indigenous slave laborers. They toiled through everything the Pacific Northwest corridor of the Mexican territory could throw at them—blinding rain, extreme heat, and intolerable cold—to complete the family dwelling, the first phase of Nueva Suiza—New Switzerland. An adobe mansion surrounded by a secure wall quickly emerged on a section of the 50,000 acres provincial Governor Alvarado had granted to Captain John Augusta Sutter, having deemed it undesirable land.

Sutter's plans expanded, as did his number of slave laborers, until an entire town, Fort Sutter, was neatly ensconced within the safety of the adobe walls. The fort was a thriving hub of industry, a rest-stop for those Canadian pioneers passing through on their way to the Salt Flats of Utah, and the captain grew restless, as he always did when things were going well. He needed more. With the addition of a sawmill, this land could become the agricultural utopia he'd envisioned when his schemes were set into play nearly seven years earlier in 1841. He would finally be the filthy rich demigod he was always meant to be. If only his abandoned wife, Anna, and their children, along with the slew of debt collectors he'd left behind in Switzerland, could see him now. He stroked his neatly groomed mustache to conceal the demented smile that crossed his lips.

"I will hold you to it, James. Before winter, we will cut trees," Sutter said, and being a man with an insatiable appetite where everything was concerned, he clapped his partner on the back in a hearty manner. "Let us partake of the fruits of mein labor."

James followed the exuberant man down the supply ramp, spying a flattened pile of horseshit with the distinct outline of his boot. He hoped the crap would wear off on the short walk to Sutter's small river-side pleasure palace, as he pondered which fruit Sutter referred. It could be anything. Food, women, whiskey, or even an exhilarating game of five-card draw. His stomach rumbled. He hoped Sutter had a thick T-bone steak in mind.

I AWAKE TO a cacophony. It echoes through the forest like the tap-tap-taps the feathered flying creatures make as they peck for sustenance upon the conifers and valley oaks aligning the riverbank. This tapping, however, is most unpleasant. A symphony of dull thuds and ground-shaking clatters.

I am not sure how long I have slept, but upon waking, I felt a distinct chill in the air. The discordant sounds erupt again and again, and I blink to view a bleak gray sky through a thin sheet of ice that has formed over my cove. It is winter. I locate the direction from which the noise originates, looking across to the other side. Something is different. A dwelling with a steep top that angles up into the clouds stands on the bank of the river.

I once met a tiny brown human, a she-child, with gentle hands and shiny coal eyes. I had been wedged beneath a cluster of river rocks for so long that I had forgotten there was an entire world outside of my rock prison. The water was shallow, and she entered my realm with such stealth and grace that I never knew she was there until the rocks above me stirred up a tornado of silty sand as she shoved them aside. She scooped her hands beneath me and lifted me towards the bright afternoon sun, baring her straight white teeth which caused me great anxiety. I had seen it all before. Sharp white teeth ripping, then eating the finned creatures who swam beneath the water. Her mouth opened, and I shut my eyes, certain I would be her next meal. What came next was not what I expected as rhythmic words flowed unencumbered from between her brown lips, and she held me close and danced me away from my rock prison. We twirled and twirled, and I grew so dizzy I was forced to close my eyes. It was only when her name drifted in on the warm summer breeze that she stopped dancing and cocked her head.

"Mariiiiaaaaahh...."

She answered in kind with a musical language that I did not understand, then kissed my golden eyelids and laid me to rest in the shallows where the river ran slowest, placing me in a mossy cove beneath the riverbank.

Though the moss in my cove has taken over the underside, it does not block my view, and I watch the brown man-humans make their music perched on beams while leaning into the angle of the framework topping the odd dwelling. This music is unlike that of the tiny brown child. This tribe of humans carries an air of defeat. Their bodies covered in tattered cloth as they beat their steady tempo—rhythms of despair. Their music-makers gleam silver when they swing an arc in the bright light of the winter sun, and I take pause to ponder.

I have seen the comings and goings of many species native to my homeland. Those creatures with whom I share these waters are covered in scales or fins and even shell-houses, and when they sleep beneath the river's cozy banks, the close proximity of their bodies to mine comforts me.

Those covered in feathers fly and nest high in the branches of the willows and pines, some hunting in darkness and others in daylight, while those covered in fur, creep or crawl to the edge of the river to drink and sometimes eat their fill before moving on.

The tribe appears when the daylight is longer than the darkness. They are quiet. A gathering of humans in various sizes and shapes who work as one to erect conical structures in which to temporarily dwell. They pay homage to the land, taking from the river and forests only what they need to survive, and when the long darkness draws near, they fold up their structures and silently move on.

My eyes scour the structure across the river to take note of its wide range of features. This dwelling is unlike any other. It is long and narrow and topped with a sloped cover to seal out the elements. A bulky box when compared to the sleekness of the temporary homes in which the traveling humans of the forest reside. It has an air of permanence. It will not easily fold to move with the shifting seasons. Again I wonder how much time had passed during my rest, as this monstrosity wasn't there before I closed my eyes. I spy a large wheel beneath the strange home. It is surrounded by a low wall of river rocks, and I watch the flow of the water and the wheel as it turns. I am hypnotized by its perpetual motion. Round and round it goes, and the dwelling's jarring thuds fade into the background as my eyelids grow heavy.

———————◆———————

A HASTILY CONSTRUCTED stage was set in the foreground of Sutter's Mill, and a hired stringed quartet shivered beneath the sliver of shelter it provided. Wind gusted as the four musicians removed the fur-lined gloves keeping their hands pliable and began to tune their instruments. The crowd was rowdy for it was out of the ordinary for an event of such magnitude to take place in January when a dusting of snow covered the ground.

Food and ale aplenty were provided at no cost to the townsfolk in celebration of the completion of the sawmill. Those who had money or something to barter would be able to witness the magic of the water-powered saw, and a line began to form at the wheelhouse entry ramp. From there, it wound around the shivering musicians on stage plucking at their strings, then snaked between tables of food and buskers frantically hawking their wares, all at prices that could not be beat, of course. It finally ended on the downwind side of the latrine ditches, alongside a second much shorter line of shifty-eyed men looking to blow off steam in the brothel. Nostrils were pinched shut against the horrific smells, and the folks at the back of both lines, each headed for a different kind of experience, attempted to not breathe which quickly became a breath-holding contest. The men in wait for the brothel relaxed, their eyes becoming less shifty, as they bonded for a moment with the sawmill folks over the misery of the stench and sounds emanating from behind a wall of bushes. But then both lines moved, in opposite directions to where fresher air reigned, and the brothel men's eyes grew shifty again while the sawmill people looked away huffing their distaste.

<hr />

THE SAWMILL TOUR started with a dark-skinned young man wearing a new set of clothes. Despite the raw chill in the air, beads of sweat formed on his forehead as he stood next to the lengthy sash-saw blade. It was the boy's job to demonstrate how the unusual vertical blade worked. A compact man named Smitty hosted the tour, repeating the same rehearsed speech over the course of several hours to awestruck townsfolk lumped together in groups of eight.

"If you turn to look left, you will see how the river flows at its natural pace," Smitty paused on every tour, to allow each grouping of eight lunkheads to work out which way was left before he continued.

"Follow the flow downstream and see how the water is redirected through the man-made narrow jetty...." He pointed. "It is this transition, from wide river to narrow jetty, that speeds up the flow giving the moving water enough force to blast the paddles of the wheel. See how rapidly the wheel spins?" Every gaze shifted downward to look through gaps in the floorboards at the wooden hurdy-gurdy wheel spinning beneath them.

"The spin of the wheel powers the pitman arm, which in turn powers the sash-saw blade. If you would be so kind, Paul...." Smitty looked at Paul, who pointed out the pitman arm first and then the blade.

"Let's hear it for Paul," Smitty bellowed as he and the frightened boy took a bow, receiving a smattering of applause for their efforts.

Then, every group had the same reaction. They looked to Paul, with expectation, for the final part of the show. Paul was barely visible as he stood behind the large blade in a slump-shouldered stance. This boy was not important. There were dozens more just like him who could fill his shoes and wear the new set of clothes. He was actually the second Paul of the day. The first had met with an unfortunate accident. His right index finger was severed by the working blade, dropping through a crack in the floorboards, only to be swept downstream. Paul number two was smaller and the heavily starched shirt hung loose on his thin body, a spot of blood barely noticeable on the cuff of his right sleeve. He stared at the floor, sweat rolling down his face, until Smitty flipped a switch setting the saw in motion. The boy launched into action, shoving his sleeves up past his elbows hiding the blossom of red. He sent log upon log through the vertical blade and debarked boards emerged on the opposite side. They were deposited into a sturdy wooden chute and slid to an area of dry ground below. The eight looked down again to watch the wheel at work, then back at the sweaty young man, all the while the logs roared through the blade. This Paul was nimble—knew to keep his fingers out of harm's way—and this demonstration continued for the awed and slack-jawed groups of eight until the light faded with the setting sun.

Marshall later noted how money and goods had exchanged hands at the sawmill and the brothel all day long, not surprised that Sutter had concocted another way to line his deep pockets.

JAMES W. MARSHALL never considered himself a digger, but that would be his fate, at least for the unforeseeable future. A covert digger, digging trenches in the dead of night through never-ending heat and rain and sleet and snow, while the rest of the population of the Pacific Northwest slept. In the wee hours of the morning, after the best danged party to have ever graced the grounds of Fort Sutter, James discovered a puddle that was steadily becoming a lake, flooding the grounds surrounding the wheelhouse. He sat down on what was possibly the only dry log between Sutter's kingdom and his distant birthplace in Hopewell, New Jersey, to have a good think. Sure as shit, this would shut down operations at Sutter's Mill, and he would catch an earful from the big man himself.

He studied the growing puddle. It hadn't taken long for him to figure out the problem. The drainage ditch was too narrow to handle the massive quantities of water draining away from the wheel. So this would be James' new life, hiding the malfunction of the mill while he solved the riddle of the puddle, and he was none too happy, but knew he would reap the rewards of a job well done—eventually. He just had to bide his time and find a solution. Be patient.

James finished the swill that passed for coffee in this uncouth land and got busy digging. The sun was rising and the early-shift workers would soon arrive. It would be best to do his work at night to keep up the illusion that all was under control and running smooth in the sawmill. So, he would dig at night, catching some shut-eye in daylight hours until something better came along or his luck changed. James dipped the cutting edge of his shovel in the river to rinse off the mud and muck when a gleam tucked away under the mossy bank on the opposite side caught his eye. He dropped the shovel and waded across the shallows to investigate.

<hr />

CAPTAIN JOHN AUGUSTUS Sutter was a cruel, self-centered man who had failed at every turn with his harebrained schemes and ventures.

He would not fail again. His eyes took on the hooded appearance of a viper as he looked down at the shiny rock held in the palm of James Marshall's hand. Despite the heavy cloud cover of the gray winter sky, two flecks, like eyes, sparkled extra bright in the muted sunlight. He felt it deep within his bones. This rock with its golden eyes would be the beginning of the end of Nueva Helvetia and his reign of brutality in this godforsaken land.

Sutter's right hand nonchalantly sifted through his coat pocket, settling upon his folding-knife. His temples throbbed with each beat of his heart as he weighed his options. Quick as a rabbit, he could put the tip of his blade through the center of one of James' devoted eyes and roll him into the river. His carcass would be swept downstream—devoured by the critters of the night before anyone was the wiser. He tightened his grip on the knife and hesitated as he struggled with his decision. Sutter clenched his teeth and pulled the hand from his pocket—empty.

"Let us keep this a secret only between the two of us, mein friend." Sutter extended his hand palm up.

As expected, Marshall nodded his reply, dropped the shiny rock into Sutter's palm, and went back to digging. Sutter had a sinking feeling he would come to regret this little act of mercy.

NO MATTER HOW long I sleep, the sky is always the same when I awaken. Heavily textured plaster—the color of the silt lining the bottom of my river—viewed above through a thin veil of glass. I was torn from my home beneath the riverbank as I slept. Scooped from my cozy cove in the shallowest part of the water to be cast into a glass vial that fit in the palm of a pale-faced human's hand. I changed hands many times, carried through arid desert, and over frosty mountaintops that led to valleys of despair littered with bones of the dead. Speeding through towns on an iron horse, faster than any man on horseback could travel, until one day, I reached my new home.

On some days, I hear how I was the first flake, the demise of a pale-faced human's legacy, but I don't understand what that means. I have always been a peaceful creature who would never harm anyone.

On other days, the story of my origin is read aloud in many voices. Over and over again, the words, engraved for all to see on the informational bronze plaque affixed to the base of my prison, are repeated with no regard as to how my world has changed.

Gold nugget. 1848.
Smithsonian's National Museum of American History.

"This small piece of yellow metal is believed to be the first piece of gold discovered in 1848 at Sutter's Mill in California, launching the gold rush."

They forgot to mention my intelligence and insightful golden eyes. I am so distraught. I was always only meant to be a creature of the river. That is all I know, and I whisper the name of my tiny brown human, Mariah. But there are no breezes in my world and her name sticks to the glass. I squeeze my eyes shut, vowing to never open them again, but no one notices.

—Lisa H. Owens, a former 1970's Egg & Spoon Bareback Horsemanship event champion and Rodeo Arena Assistant in an underwhelming Florida Panhandle redneck roping circuit, resides in North Texas with two rescue dogs and a division of dying houseplants. She began writing when she was 56, her first published story being a horror-memoir about the time she was nearly abducted by Ted Bundy at a shady motel in Pensacola Florida in 1978. Her stories and poems have been featured in a multitude of anthologies and on ezines, some of which include: Globe Soup, Black Hare Press Patreon, Black Ink Fiction, The Drabble, 100-Word Story, 101 Words, The World of Myth Magazine, Spillwords, WOW! (Women on Writing), Horror Tree's Dark Nowhere Series, Short Story Avenue, The NZ Dream,

Short Story Town, Coping Magazine *and narrated on podcasts* Scare you to Sleep, Weird Christmas, Creepy Pod, *and* The Poet's Lounge. *Lisa's work sometimes earns a nod in writing competitions and she has nearly two hundred publications to date in various genres, her favorites being dark comedy. Most stories are inspired by true events, often including private jokes and family secrets. You can read samples of her work at www.lisahowens.com.*

A GUN CALLED SINNER

M. BRANDON ROBBINS

LOGAN COOPER STEPPED on a twig as he approached Clay Wilson's camp. He cursed himself for the error. If Clay was quick enough, he could put a bullet in him before Logan had a chance to act. Sure enough, the horse thief pulled his pistol and whirled around to face Logan. Logan held his rifle level at Clay, who—much to Logan's surprise—was holding his fire. Maybe the outlaw wanted to try and talk his way out of his predicament.

"Evenin', Clay," Logan said, his voice as calm and relaxed as if the two men weren't holding guns on each other.

"Evenin'," Clay answered. "Kind of sloppy announcing your presence like that."

"No difference. Not like I was going to shoot you in the back anyway."

"Much appreciated." Clay bowed his head with genuine thanks and respect.

"Don't mention it."

"Well, it seems we've got a bit of an impasse, don't we?"

"Hardly. My gun's bigger and more accurate. I believe I'd win if we started shooting at each other."

"You probably would. But see, I'm not too keen on going to jail.

So, why don't you back away slowly, and we won't have to see who wins or loses?"

"Can't do that, Clay. You're worth an awful lot of money."

"Is that so?"

"Yep. Eight hundred."

Clay laughed. "Hell, son, I've got more than that back home. What say you meet up with me a week from now at Lando's and I pay you nine-fifty to forget this ever happened."

"No can do. I've got my reputation to uphold."

Nothing was said between the two men for several moments. Then Clay broke the silence again.

"Hell." He lowered the hammer on his pistol and pitched it toward Logan. "You've still got to get me to town if you want to collect that bounty. Who's to say I won't talk some sense into you?"

Logan, still keeping his gun trained on Clay, stooped to pick up the pistol. "This all you got?"

"There's a shotgun in the holster on my saddle." He nodded towards his horse. Logan kept his gun aimed at Clay while circling around to the animal, drawing the shotgun with one hand. Still holding his rifle, he opened it to eject the two shells inside and slid it back inside the holster.

Clay turned back to his fire. Its glow increased in intensity as the sun faded in the sky and night took over the open range. "Was just about to make some coffee and fry up some sowbelly. Interested?"

Logan came to sit at Clay's side—never taking his hand off his rifle. "I could eat."

———————

AFTER A BREAKFAST of cold biscuits, salt pork, and hot coffee—this meal provided by Logan—the bounty hunter freed Clay's feet from the shackles holding them so he would be able to mount his horse.

"You could take the cuffs off of my wrists too," Clay said, holding up his hands. "I promise to behave myself," he said with the mocking sincerity of a mischievous schoolboy.

Logan did not acknowledge him.

"Now, how am I supposed to ride a horse without a full range of motion in my upper limbs?" Clay asked with mock concern in his voice.

Logan saddled up his own horse. "Very carefully," he answered. "Or, you can walk."

Clay smirked and pulled himself up onto his saddle. "Lead the way, good sir."

They had been riding together for about an hour when the outlaw finally broke the silence between them.

"So, Logan, is it true what they say about your guns? That you've named them?"

"Not so much as named but just given myself some reminders of who and what I am."

"And what's that?"

"Something you would no doubt identify with."

"I say again—what's that?"

Logan huffed and shook his head. "I see that I will have to bargain with you as one does with a child. If I tell you, will you stop this line of questioning?"

"I won't if you don't."

"I've got the word 'sinner' carved on the grip of my pistol and 'unforgiven' on the stock of my rifle."

Clay whistled and raised an eyebrow. "Mighty dark and heavy thoughts you've got there."

"Well, I've done some things for which I don't rightly feel I've atoned."

"Anything you mind sharing?"

"You a preacher? This confession?"

"Speaking as someone who has done his own share of unforgivable sins, I can attest that confession is good for the soul, whether to a preacher or a fellow sinner."

Logan huffed and shrugged his shoulders. "I was in the Army for a spell. Took some lives that didn't need taking."

"You said it yourself. You were in the Army. You were just following orders."

"Doesn't mean I don't feel accountable for what I did. Now, we've had a good talk. What do you say we enjoy some quiet contemplation, maybe a little silent prayer?"

Clay smirked and rolled his eyes skyward. "Lord," he shouted out. "Forgive this sinner you see before you, and forgive Logan Cooper, who makes a living turning free men over to be chained or hanged or otherwise given to the care of the sovereign state for time indetermin-able. Wash his hands of blood and his soul of dirt and—"

Logan struck him in the jaw with the butt of his pistol, silencing him for a moment before Clay spat out blood and laughed through reddened lips. "That's a mighty heavy firearm there, Cooper."

"You trying to get in my head, Clay, just know you won't like what you find there."

The two men rode the rest of the day in silence, save for an occa-sional hymn that Clay chose to sing out loud, which Logan did nothing to silence.

LOGAN SHARED A can of beans with Clay. They ate their supper by the campfire, and Logan sipped on a flask of bourbon between bites.

"Ya know," Clay said after swallowing his last bit of beans, "a sip of that bourbon would hit the spot."

"Yeah, I just bet it would." Logan took a long draw from his flask and gobbled up the rest of his beans.

Clay snorted in exaggerated contempt and helped himself to a swig from the water canteen Logan had handed him at the start of their meal. When he was done with it, Logan reached a hand out. Clay gave it to him and he watched the bounty hunter knock back a swallow to chase his bourbon.

"So, Logan, you thought any more about my offer?"

"I have not."

"Would it help you think if I made it twelve hundred?"

"No, it would not."

"How about fifteen? That's more than enough to set you up in a grand way. Get you a new horse, some new clothes, maybe a bit of land. You could take up farming. Wouldn't need to bloody your hands anymore. Don't that sound more like a calling for a man who needs redeeming?"

"I grew up farming. Not much for it. I don't have a mind for making things grow."

"So invest some in a business. Buy out that hotel in Parkersville. That's where you stay, right? Parkersville? Nice town, so I hear. You could maybe take up a partnership in the casino or the cat house. Hell, just sit on the money for all I care. You'd be richer than most men could ever hope to be."

"You sure are in a hurry to be separated from your money, Clay."

"It's not like I can take it with me when I'm gone, and if you turn me in, I'll be gone in no time flat. How's that make you feel, Logan, knowing that you're leading me to my death?"

"You chose to steal horses and kill men, Clay. Same as the rest of your gang. You've dug your own hole."

"Those people you killed in times of war made their choices too, Cooper. Why the regret and despair over them but not me?"

Logan took a deep breath and slid his hat off. He ran his fingers through his shaggy hair, took another sip of bourbon, and started speaking. "In the war, my company met up with this Union outfit on the road. Seems we were both marching to the same place, taking different routes, and stopped to camp just a few miles apart. We scattered out into the woods, taking up positions behind cover, hoping to get the drop on them. They had the same idea. We started skirmishing after a bit, then fighting for real, and after a while we were running low on ammo so we set our bayonets and charged them.

"Now, they should have ripped us to shreds. They were better equipped, had more rounds, and were probably better fed. But I guess we scared the sweet Hell out of them, because by the time we got to their front lines, they were all on their knees with their hands up in the air."

Clay asked, "So, what happened then?"

Logan stared into the fire. His face weary with the memory of blood and screams. "We ran those poor sons of bitches through to the last one. Our officers cut them down with their swords. They shot the few who tried to run away with their pistols. They fought back, but they weren't prepared to. It was like pigs to the slaughter. We killed every last boy in blue."

"Damn, Logan. That's cold."

"I remember one of them looked up at me while he bled to death on my bayonet, and said, 'Tell Mama I love her.' I don't remember what I said back to him."

Clay snorted and spat. "Why you telling me this?"

"I could tell in his eyes that he didn't want to be there. And not just in the way that none of us really wanted to be fighting. No, this young man had been called up. He had not volunteered. He just wanted to do his time and get back home. And I killed him. So forgive me if I don't have much sympathy for somebody who chose to be a horse thief and a killer."

Clay shook his head. "My mama was a whore, Logan. I don't know who my daddy was. My mother died when I was seven, and I was raised by the rest of the girls. I never went to school, wasn't fit for the army, had no skills to speak of. I knew how to fight, and I knew how to shoot, and I knew that horses fetch a pretty penny. So, do you really think I had a choice?"

Logan took another drink of bourbon. "I do. If you had sought it out, you would have found a way to make an honest living."

"Honest livings don't get men much of anywhere."

Logan leaned back on his bedroll and tilted his hat to cover his eyes. "G'night, Clay. See you in the morning."

***

LOGAN WAS STOMPING out the fire the next morning when two men came riding hard from the road to their campsite, sliding down from their horses as they approached at breakneck speed. They had their guns drawn when they yelled for Logan to put his hands up. Clay greeted them with a hearty laugh.

"Took y'all long enough!" Clay said.

Logan did not raise his hands but drew his pistol, holding it level at the two newcomers, floating his aim from one to the other. "Friends of yours, Clay?"

"Oh, closer than friends and tighter than brothers! These here are two of my boys in the gang."

One of them spoke up. "We rode all night to catch up with you, boss. We ain't slept a wink."

Logan eyed them both in turn. "Fellas, why don't we put our guns up and we have a nice talk?"

The other man now offered a reply. "Ain't no need to talk! We don't want to shoot you, Cooper, seeing as how you didn't shoot the boss. But we will shoot you if we have to."

"Yeah," his partner snapped. "Don't think you're in any place to be negotiating right now."

"Look now, boys," Logan said, "you're tired. Your reflexes are slow. You won't be able to outshoot me."

"We'll shoot you dead before you can blink!" The first man gritted his teeth.

"Want to bet your life you're faster than me?" Logan responded.

There was the briefest of moments where everything came to a standstill before the shooting started. Logan dropped to one knee. As he hit the ground, Logan fired off two rounds. The first hit one outlaw square between the eyes. The second punched through the other's jaw and exited through the back of his head. They were both dead before they hit the ground.

The reports of the pistol shots were still echoing in the air when Clay kicked Logan in the back of the head, knocking him over and causing him to drop his pistol. Clay leapt forward and wrapped the chains of his shackles around Logan's throat, pinning him to the ground with his knee. Logan reached desperately for his gun, but it was just out of his reach.

Logan started flailing backwards with his elbow, trying to hit his opponent in the side and knock him off of his back. He finally succeeded just as he started to black out from a lack of air. Logan crawled toward his pistol and reclaimed it. He cocked it and spun to face Clay, who was lunging for him once more. The outlaw pinned the bounty hunter back to the ground, forcing the chains into Logan's throat. Logan jammed the muzzle of the pistol against Clay's side.

"Give it up," Logan gasped out as he pressed his gun into Clay's ribs.

"You bring me in, it'll have to be cold," Clay responded through gritted teeth. He pressed the chain of the shackles deeper into Logan's throat. The bounty hunter turned red from lack of air.

Logan pulled the trigger sending a round into Clay's rib cage and up into his lungs.

Clay fell over, leaving Logan to gasp for air. The outlaw started wheezing. A pink foam formed on his lips. Logan worked into a sitting position and turned to face his bounty.

"Am I dying?" Clay whispered.

"I'm afraid so."

Clay smiled weakly. "How about some of that bourbon?"

Logan went to his horse and retrieved the flask from his pack. He returned to Clay and poured a little of the alcohol into his mouth. The outlaw choked it down and smiled without sincerity once more. "Tell mama I love her." He coughed, groaned, and breathed one last time.

The bounty hunter ran his finger over the inscription on the grip of his pistol, tracing every letter of the word *"SINNER"* before holstering the gun. He took a deep sigh, helped himself to a swig of bourbon, and set about hoisting Clay's body onto his horse.

—M. Brandon Robbins is a writer from North Carolina, where he still lives. He holds a Bachelor of Arts in English from the University of Mount Olive and a Master of Library Science from East Carolina University. He wrote the "Games, Gamers, and Gaming" column for Library Journal *from 2012-2017.*

His fiction has appeared in Shotgun Horror Clips, Trembling With Fear, *and* Rope and Wire. *Brandon's chapbook, "Heart of Stone," was published as part of Demain Publishing's* Short Sharp Shocks! *series. His blog,* Writing Screams, *can be found at writingscreams.blog. Brandon works full-time as a school librarian. When he's not writing, he enjoys reading, gaming, watching movies, and listening to music. Brandon works primarily in the horror genre, but has a healthy appreciation for westerns and writes one from time to time. Growing up, there was a western on TV every Sunday afternoon. He's been a fan ever since, and to this day watches reruns of* The Rifleman *with his mother-in-law.*

The Chase by Charles Marion Russell

LITTLE-BURNT-ALL-OVER

MERLE DAVENPORT

ON THE SHORES of Lake Otsego, long before the White man came, lived a hunter, strong and mighty, with his wife and only daughter. By day, the girl worked beside her mother learning to cut and clean the game her father brought home, to turn the hides into buckskin and sew them together using porcupine needles, to mend the nets, and keep the birch-bark canoe from leaking.

As they worked, her mother taught her the legends and songs of her people. Her favorite time of each day was when her mother took her to the shores of the lake to watch the Lord of the Sky walk into the west so the stars could have their time to shine.

"Where does the sun go at night?" she asked her mother.

"He has other villages to visit with his glory. They need to see his face as much as we do."

"Then why do the colors follow the sun before the night comes?"

"During the day, his face is so bright you cannot see his headdress. But, when he disappears into the west, you can see the rainbow that he wears on his head."

The little girl thought about this and smiled—glad that the Lord of the Sky gave them so much beauty to lift their burdens at the end of the day.

"Mother, why are there lights in the night after the sun disappears?"

"Ah, that is the purple robe of the Lord of the Sky. He carries the *wampum* beads of our people on his robe."

"*Wampum* beads?"

"Our people have known trouble in the past. Each time we rise above our troubles and renew our faith, a *wampum* bead appears on his great robe. The greater the trouble, the brighter the bead on his cloak."

"I don't understand."

"It is our spirit that makes us strong, not our bows. We were the first to be given the fire because we understood that it is our inner spirit, not the strength of our arms, that makes us into skilled warriors and hunters."

The daughter nodded her head and gazed into the night sky. She marveled at all the beads that covered the sky from horizon to horizon. It was a comfort to know that no matter what she faced in her life, the Lord of the Sky would always be there to give her strength.

One evening when they watched the sunset, the daughter noticed that her mother was quieter than normal.

"Why are you troubled, mother?"

"I fear I am not going to be with you much longer. I have a sickness that I will not survive."

The daughter's lip trembled, and her eyes welled with tears.

"Before I go, I must tell you of the vision I was given when you were born. My dream showed me that you will face trials like no other in our village has ever known. If you bear them with patience and refuse to give in to bitterness, then you will be honored above all other maidens. Remember to trust in the Lord of the Sky. When your time of trouble begins, he will give you the strength you need to bear it."

Afraid to trust her voice, the girl nodded and threw her arms around her mother.

"Don't forget to keep your spirit pure so that your *wampum* bead will shine brightly in the sky."

Three days later, the village carried her mother's body to the sacred burial grounds and laid her to rest. The little girl and her father both mourned their loss. She recalled all the skills she learned and all the lessons she had been taught by her mother. Though the *wigwam* was well cared for, her father never seemed to smile anymore.

As summer was turning into fall, her father decided to marry a widow who had two daughters. Villagers raised their voices in approval. Although the girl sang her approval as well, she was doubtful that her new mother would bring harmony to the *wigwam*. To make matters worse, her two daughters were lazier than a snake baking in the warm afternoon sun.

Images of her mother came to the girl's mind. She had warned of a time of trouble. Perhaps this was her time.

"Don't worry, mother," she said to the sky, "I'll keep my spirit pure so that my *wampum* bead will shine brightly next to yours in the sky."

The two older girls soon discovered that the youngest was the best cook. Rather than help with the daily meals, they were happy to have her do all the cooking. They also had her catch the fish, tan the hides, and gather nuts and berries. When she was done with that, she had to make them new moccasins and dresses and decorate them with animal bones and porcupine quills.

Anytime that she didn't do exactly what her older sisters said they would beat her with the nearest stick they could find. Sometimes they chose a flaming stick from the fire which burned her skin and scorched her clothes. Before long, old scars and fresh welts covered her body from head to toe. She was burned so often her sisters laughed at her and called her Little Burnt-All-Over.

Every time they beat her, she remembered her mother's words, *"Bear your trials with patience and do not give in to bitterness."* Her faith in the Lord of the Sky gave her strength to never become cruel like her sisters.

For years, Little Burnt-All-Over suffered at the hands of her cruel sisters. Every imagined wrong, every invented insult, was blamed on her. Night after night, she went to sleep with fresh bruises, singed hair, and blisters from the hot coals. Night after night, she gazed into the night sky to see the *wampum* beads of her people reminding her that others had suffered to make them a great nation.

One morning, a runner arrived in her village with great news. He said that a mighty hunter had built a white lodge at the other end of the lake.

"He is here to choose a bride from our village," he announced to the great delight of all the maidens.

Little Burnt-All-Over dropped her head in shame. She knew that the great lord would never want to choose someone who was as scarred and disfigured as she was. He deserved the best that the village offered, not the ugliest.

"Help me get ready, Little Burnt-All-Over," demanded the oldest sister. "I am going to the end of the lake to meet this mighty hunter and become his bride."

She put on her best dress and moccasins while Little Burnt-All-Over oiled her hair until it shone. After she braided the girl's hair, she used some of her own sea shells to decorate the ends of her braids.

"You look beautiful," commented Little Burnt-All-Over with a smile. "I'm sure he will choose you as a bride."

"He better or I'll beat you," threatened the sister.

That evening, the oldest daughter returned angry that she had not been chosen as a bride. She grasped a burning stick from the fire and beat Little Burnt-All-Over senseless.

The next morning, the second daughter went to the white lodge to marry the mighty warrior from far away. She rummaged through what was left of Little Burnt-All-Over's shells and took them for her own. After all, if the older sister was not chosen, it must be because she was not beautiful enough to catch the great lord's eye.

With the help of Little Burnt-All-Over, the middle sister put on her best dress, decorated with shells and quills.

"You didn't braid and grease my hair properly!" she shouted at Little Burnt-All-Over when she returned. The middle sister picked up a stick out of the fire and began beating Little Burnt-All-Over. Hot coals from the flaming wood burned her face and hair. Seeing that the middle sister was not chosen as a bride either, the oldest sister picked another stick out of the fire and beat her as well. Little Burnt-All-Over tried to protect herself from the rage of her two sisters, but it did no good. By the time they stopped beating her, she was bleeding from a dozen places and burnt in a dozen more.

"Mother, help me," she cried out in despair. "I have no place to go. You said to bear my torments with grace, but I can no longer endure their beatings. They are so angry they will kill me if I return. Even if I go to another village, they will not accept me. No one wants an ugly, scarred woman."

That night, the rainbow headdress of the Lord of the Sky was more brilliant than she had ever seen. Colors and hues shone brightly as his great shining face disappeared over the horizon. Even the stars looked closer and brighter than ever as his rich purple robe filled the night sky. All the *wampum* beads shone so brightly she thought she could reach out and take them in her hand.

"One day, my *wampum* bead will shine in the sky. I know that the Great Spirit has seen my suffering at the hands of my sisters. I know he will place my bead up there with our ancestors."

"I know I can't live in this village any longer," she mumbled to herself. "Perhaps I will visit the White Lodge at the end of the lake. Perhaps they have need of a servant to cook and clean for them. I will work hard if they give me a place to stay."

By the time she arrived at the hide door of the lodge, it was nearly mid-afternoon. Cautiously, she scratched on the hide afraid that no one would answer.

"Good morning, child," said an old woman, pulling aside the hide flap. "If you come to see my son, he is not here. He has gone to prepare for his bride, but he will return soon."

"Oh, I'm too ugly to be his bride. I only came to ask how I may serve you in his lodge."

The old woman laughed so joyfully. that Little Burnt-All-Over smiled despite herself.

"Why don't you go down the eastern trail? Then come back and tell me what you saw."

"As you wish, Grandmother."

When she reached the top of a hill, she saw a mighty chief walking toward her. Even though she knew she had never met him, somehow he looked familiar as if she had known him all her life.

As the great chief drew near, Little Burnt-All-Over dropped her eyes, grateful that she had seen him in all his glory. After he passed by, she ran back to the lodge.

"What did you see, dear child?"

"At first, I saw a man with eagle feathers in his hair. Then I realized it was not feathers, it was a rainbow and the face, which was so easy to see before, became too bright to look at, as if I was looking at the sun."

"What did he have in his hand?"

"At first, I thought it was a bow. Then I realized it was a mighty storm cloud and his arrows were jagged bolts of lightning."

"In his other hand?"

"He had two enormous black dogs. They were strange dogs, each with one eye in the middle of his forehead. They were the Black Dogs of Winter who come when the white wind makes ready for a storm."

"Did you see anything else?"

"On his shoulders, he wore a great purple mantle covered with shining *wampum* beads."

"Blessed are you among all women for you have truly seen my son!" said the old woman with great delight. "Don't you know why my son came to this lake?"

"To find a bride from my village."

"Not just any bride. He came here to find you."

"Me? Why would he search for a poor scarred girl he has never met?"

"Oh, my dear child. My son knows you very well. It was he who watched over you every evening when you came to the lake to watch him pass beyond the horizon. Every time you stared at the *wampum* of his purple mantle, he dreamed of the day when you would become his bride."

"But I am scarred and burned. A great chief like your son should have a wife who is young and beautiful, not one who is ugly and bruised."

Without warning, the great chief walked up to the lodge. "My dearest

Little Burnt-All-Over," said the great chief, stepping into the doorway. "The true beauty of a maiden is not in her body. It is in her spirit. Skin wrinkles and hair turns gray, but a pure spirit remains bright forever."

"How can you know my spirit when we've never met?"

The great chief gazed deeply in Little Burnt-All-Over's eyes until she recognized him.

"You... you're the Lord of the Sky!"

"I first saw you as a little girl, sitting at your mother's side by the lake," explained the Lord of the Sky. "You loved the colors of my passing and fell in love with the shining wampum beads of my mantle. It was then that I knew you would become my bride."

"Yes," she replied as she saw the same love in his eyes that she had always felt when she gazed into the night sky. "Yes, I know you now. I have always known you."

"Long have I watched you and waited for your time of trial and suffering to be complete. Many times, I wished I could save you from your cruel beatings. Every time your spirit overcame the anger and hate of your sisters, I rejoiced. Each victory made your spirit shine brighter. And now that your time of trial is over, I have come to claim you as my bride."

"I don't understand."

"Most call me the Lord of the Sky, but I am also known as the King of the Day. Until now, I had no bride, no Queen to rule the Night." The chief took the purple mantle off his shoulders and wrapped it around Little Burnt-All-Over. "Tomorrow we will be wed. Then you will rule with me forever."

"The Queen of the Night?"

"All you see now are the twinkling wampum beads of your people. Soon they will see your face shining down on them. You will be a reflection of my glory–a great light surrounded by the smaller wampum beads."

She stared in wonder at the Lord of the Sky.

"Little Burnt-All-Over, you will be my bride and wear my mantle. The King to rule the day and his Queen to rule the night. Whenever our people look into the night sky, they will see your shining face with all its scars. They will see you and know that the purest spirit shines brightest in the darkest night. It will remind them that their sorrows only serve to strengthen their spirits for all to see."

—Merle Davenport began telling stories to his children nearly thirty years ago. When they asked him to write them down, he discovered his passion for writing. Since then, he has won awards for his poetry, fantasy, non-fiction, and historical romance, but his favorite genre will always be retelling ancient myths and legends. As a transplanted Yankee, he has fallen in love with his new home state of Oklahoma where he resides with his wife and two dogs.

THIRST

MICHAEL F. MCDONNELL

THE MAN FACING him was drunk and looked like he'd been that way for a day or two. Perhaps longer.

Crenshaw was bone tired and wanted only two things—to sit on something other than a saddle and to drink something other than the tepid, sulfurous water in his canteen. If he could bathe and have his clothing washed, so much the better.

The drunken man had other ideas.

"Every man who comes to this town needs to prove himself," slurred the drunk looking down at Crenshaw from the boardwalk. "What's it going to be—fists or guns?"

"I'm not going to fight you," Crenshaw responded as he climbed the three steps. "I'm too done in, and you're too drunk so it wouldn't be much of a fight. Why don't I buy you a drink instead."

"You're gutless," muttered the drunk. "It'll be guns."

With that, the man stepped down from the boardwalk and staggered into the street where he turned and stood, feet apart, peering down the middle of the street toward something no one else could see. His knees locked and unlocked in turn causing him to jerk back and forth. It looked like he was trying to walk but couldn't get his feet to move.

His face was flaccid. His eyes were vacant. Right hand poised over his gun, he waited.

Crenshaw stood for a moment looking at the sorry excuse for a man standing in the street and half expecting him to pitch forward on his face. Crenshaw liked a drink but knew he could never end up in that state. He turned his back to the man and pushed through the batwing doors into the saloon.

The room was long and narrow with the bar on the right and tables on the left. It was dim inside. With the midday sun directly overhead little light came in through the windows flanking the door. He paused to let his eyes adjust.

Two drovers sat clutching shot glasses in dirty hands. A partial bottle of whiskey sat on the table between them.

Crenshaw walked slowly through the narrow space between the bar and the tables, keeping an eye on the two men and the bartender. At the far end, he turned and rested his left elbow on the bar and left foot on the rail.

One of the drovers, the one who now had his back to Crenshaw, moved his chair with a loud grating sound so as to be able to watch Crenshaw.

The room was still and silent for a moment before the bartender asked in a dry, raspy voice, "What'll you be having?"

"Water if it's clean. And whiskey if it's not rotgut."

"Water's outside in the trough if you want some," said the bartender. "The whiskey is fine."

The two seated men snickered.

The bartender set a bottle and a shot glass on the bar. Crenshaw grabbed them and moved to a table where he sat facing the door to the street.

"I heard you talking to Bullock outside," croaked the bartender. "If there's fighting to be done, do it out there not in here."

"I just want a drink," said Crenshaw, his own voice harsh from lack of use and the dust of the desert. "I'm not here to wrangle."
After a moment he added, "Someone ought to take that Bullock home."

No one responded.

Crenshaw filled the glass and threw the shot down his throat. He immediately poured the glass full again. Indeed, it was fine whiskey.

All four men looked to the door when they heard the hollow, uneven thump of footsteps on the boardwalk. The batwing doors parted. The man named Bullock shambled into the room.

He looked around as if unable to concentrate before his bleary eyes came to rest on Crenshaw.

"You're a coward, mister," he said loudly.

Crenshaw ignored him and downed the second shot, keeping his eyes on Bullock even with his head tipped back.

"Randall, you know there's to be no fighting inside here. Take it outside," said the bartender in such a way that Crenshaw believed it was not the first time such a thing had been said to Bullock.

"I tried that. The coward wouldn't have it."

Crenshaw had no wish to engage with any of these men. They were all hard looking. The cowpokes wore guns, and he was certain the bartender would have a shotgun tucked away but near at hand.

All Crenshaw now wanted was to have a third shot of whiskey, pay what he owed, and ride away from this place.

The man named Bullock squared himself toward Crenshaw.

"Randall, now you hold it right there," said the bartender as if speaking to a child. "There's no shooting in here. You know that. Don't make me take you outside."

Crenshaw appeared as casual as when he had first walked in. But, all his senses were alive.

He had no doubt the bartender, a large man, could easily have handled Bullock, but to get to him he'd have to either come around the open end of the bar and past Crenshaw or vault over the bar.

Bullock was swaying back and forth. His fingers wiggling above his gun. His eyes suddenly came into focus.

He made his move.

Crenshaw drew from his seated position and fired before Bullock's gun had cleared the holster. The bullet struck the drunken man's hand. His gun clattered to the floor.

Bullock made a strange sound as he looked down at his bloodied, mangled hand.

The two men at the table hadn't moved, but the bartender was now pointing a shotgun at Crenshaw.

"I said there was no fighting inside," growled the bartender.

"My hand," squealed Bullock.

"I have no quarrel with you sir," Crenshaw said politely.

"And I've none with you," said the bartender, "Now, you holster up and get out. I won't shoot unless you give me cause."

One of the drovers rose slowly. His hands out to his sides. Everyone watched him carefully as he moved to Bullock and sat him down.

"I only wanted a drink of water and to rest," said Crenshaw, "that's all."

He stood slowly and holstered.

Crenshaw moved past Bullock. The cowboy had backed up against the wall, showing his empty hands as Crenshaw passed. The second cowboy sat very still., His hands resting on the table palms up. These men knew a dangerous man when they saw one.

Crenshaw looked to his left at the bartender who still had the shotgun pointed at him.

"Now, why would you point a gun at somebody you know has no intention of shooting anyone?" he asked.

He set some coins on the bar.

The bartender lowered the shotgun, resting it across his forearm and nodded at Crenshaw.

Crenshaw crossed the boardwalk pausing on the steps. He had no fear of those inside. The bartender had passed on the chance to do him harm and would stop the others from trying if they got reckless. A small group of men clustered across the street looking his way. They all kept their distance.

Glancing at the horse trough he decided not to dunk his head in the dirty water. He looked around but saw no sign of a well.

As he rode away, he asked himself what it was that makes a man, even a drunken man, think he can do anything he pleases? What makes a man think he can bully his way to success in every dispute, challenge every man, and best him? What kind of meanness and hurt lives in a man who sets out to start a fight for no other reason than hubris?

They had both made their decisions. Bullock hadn't meant to have his hand mangled but brought that on himself. Despite being forced into doing something he didn't want to do, Crenshaw had made a difficult shot in wounding him. A far easier shot would have been to shoot at the man's chest and kill him outright.

Was he right to have engaged with Bullock? He could have got back on his horse and ridden on at the start and avoided the entire matter. He could have dived for cover or rushed at Bullock. He could have waited for Bullock to shoot first in the hope that in his state he'd miss. But only a fool would play those cards.

What is it that defines destiny, Crenshaw wondered. What happenstance had led him across the emptiness of the high plains to then crest a hill and find this isolated town surrounded by nothing but desert and mountains? What sort of people were they who populated such a place and allowed a fool to create a situation where a man was going to be harmed, whether it was the drunk himself or someone else?

He rode up out of the shallow valley, stopped at the top of a hill above the town, and looked back. He didn't even know the name of the sorry place. He hoped he never saw it again.

Riding down the reverse slope of the rise he pondered how it is that a simple decision to seek a cool drink had led to such an outcome. A man's life, and the lives of those around him, had changed because Crenshaw was thirsty and saddle sore. He would think about fate and chance as he again rode into the desert that stretched off toward the distant mountains.

He was still thirsty.

—M. F. McDonnell is a Canadian author new to writing fiction. His non-fiction work has appeared in the Hamilton Spectator *newspaper. He will have a short story published at close2thebone.co.uk in 2025.*

Surrounded by Charles Schreyvogel

SURE SHOT

PAMELA REDCLIFF

SAN JUAN MOUNTAINS
1896

AT SUCH A high elevation, the sun wasn't quite sharp enough to scald, and the breeze was bone-dry. As I worked in the vegetable garden beside our cabin, I wished for one sultry summer day like I'd known as a child in Tennessee. The air sweet with honeysuckle and sweat rolling from under my ginger braids down between my shoulders while I sipped mint tea on the porch with my grandma. I allowed my thoughts to wander as I toiled, staving off the boredom that accompanied weeding the rows. My calico bonnet shaded my eyes and prevented more freckles on my nose. I wore a long-sleeve cotton blouse to protect my pale arms, but my hands were nearly as bronzed as the sweet muscadine grapes I'd picked as a girl. My son, Lukas, was inside taking a nap.

We'd had precious little rain all summer so there weren't enough serviceberries nor chokecherries to satisfy the black bears, and a few had ventured within shouting distance of our cabin. My husband, Emil, had also seen cougar tracks on the road to town, so he urged me to keep his Winchester hunting rifle nearby whenever he worked his shift at the gold mine and I was outside alone or with Lukas. I'd be as fierce as a momma bear if any critter came near my dimple-cheeked boy.

I learned how to shoot soon after we moved here five years ago. Down below the cabin, Emil set up bottles on the hillside. We stood back a ways, and he raised the rifle and fired. The blast resounded in my ears. He shot a couple more rounds so I'd get the idea. When it was my turn, I cocked the lever and lifted the rifle to my shoulder—surprised by how heavy and cumbersome it felt. I aimed at one of the bottles and squeezed the trigger. The butt of the gun punched my shoulder like a drunken bully, and I stumbled backward into Emil's arms. He smoothed over my embarrassment with his kisses and laughter. We now joked that my aim was darn near as sharp as his.

Emil and I met in Cripple Creek when I worked as a faro dealer at the Silver Chance Saloon. My best friend, Juanita, one of the saloon's soiled doves, enticed me outside one Christmas Eve during a snowstorm to make snowballs and recall our happier times as children. Snowflakes the size of silver dollars tumbled down through the light of the streetlamps, and everything was clean and white. Several young men streamed out of the beer garden next to the Silver Chance, and Juanita and I were caught in the crossfire of their snowball fight. When she joined in and landed a snowball in the back of one young man, he spun around to return fire. She jumped out of the way leaving me an open target. I had no time to react as the snowball struck my face with ice-cold sharpness followed by scorching fire. That was the first time I laid eyes on Emil Bonner, and I haven't wanted to lose sight of him since. On our wedding night, I told him the shiner he gave me with the snowball was well worth it.

As newlyweds, we traveled by train to Lake City through steep canyons and alongside rushing rivers capped white with rapids. At times, we barreled through the mountain itself, and I clung to Emil— fear and excitement colliding inside of me. We had big plans. I hoped to one day own a restaurant in town while my blue-eyed German with a hawklike brow intended to strike it rich as a prospector. To pass the time on the train ride, he told me of the riches the mountains held and described our new home on Tower Creek where he had staked his claim and built a cabin for us.

I should've been exhausted after the train ride to Lake City and the rough buggy ride to our cabin, but the stunning views of stone peaks jutting above blue-green valleys were like gifts opening themselves to me. Embraced by such beauty and beginning a new life with the man I loved, I'd never been happier.

"We have but a single neighbor," he told me on the buggy ride. "Her name is Mahala Collins. She's a widow who has lived there many years."

"By herself in the mountains?"

"Yes, and she's excited to meet you, Maggie. She kept an eye on me from her porch all summer as I built our cabin. Says she's a healer. Whatever that is."

"I haven't heard that term since I was a girl. Means she cures people using herbs and natural concoctions."

"That's good since we don't have a doctor nearby."

When we arrived at the cabin, the elderly woman with a dark complexion and tight ringlets of salt and pepper hair waved to us from her porch. I waved back as Emil caught me by surprise, sweeping me out of the buggy and bounding up the steps with me in his arms. He wrestled open the door and spun me around giving me a full-circle view of our new home. As light as the air, I floated.

Such a beautiful memory, I thought as I yanked at the bindweed that was attempting to climb the cornstalks. Life became more complicated after that.

I soon discovered my charming husband had painted a too rosy picture of our future and the place where I envisioned one day living. The founders of Lake City deemed it the "metropolis" of the San Juan Mountains. A laughable description given its smattering of residents and handful of shops. The town lacked most of the amenities I'd enjoyed in Cripple Creek and certainly wouldn't support the restaurant I had in mind where I cooked up my specialties and served them on tables covered with white linen.

"Don't worry," Emil had told me when I expressed my disappointment. "The town will grow. It has a railroad now, and the silver and gold will bring more people."

"I hope so. As much as I love our cabin, I can't wait to live in town and share my recipes with more than one customer." I gave him a wink.

"You know how I love your cooking." He'd pulled me into his arms and nuzzled my neck with his whiskered cheek. "It'll happen. Please be patient—with the town and me."

After I discovered I was with child, I tucked my plans in my pocket, and we prepared to start a family. Then life knocked us off the pin we'd been dancing on. I miscarried. On our saddest day, we buried our daughter near Mahala's husband. When we moved here, I never considered we'd need a cemetery.

Mahala and her husband had arrived at Tower Creek in 1875. They had hopes of their own—of a peaceful life where skin color didn't matter. What town couldn't use a respectable smithy and a self-taught healer? Mahala never intended to become a hermit, but that's what happened after her husband was killed by a kick from a feisty mare at his blacksmith shop in Lake City. A few townsfolk continued to venture out this way for her cures, though some believed she was a witch. I knew otherwise. She was from East Tennessee, same as me, so we bonded from the start. After I lost the baby, Mahala became my guardian angel. I welcomed her soothing teas and steady consolation.

"A woman should have another woman to lean on during this sorrowful time," she told me. "So, honey, you can lean on me."

Every day that summer, I made a pilgrimage to my daughter's grave along a path lined with purple columbines, fiery Indian paintbrush, bluebells, and lupine. Mahala had taught me the names of the wildflowers which lay all around me like a color-splashed carpet. I admired their resilience—buried for months beneath the winter snow yet reappearing every summer undaunted. What courageous little souls they had, so much braver than mine. As I walked, I'd pick the prettiest, adding a few bright orange lilies which Mahala said were a symbol of motherhood and rebirth. I'd place them in my basket as I hummed "Wayfaring Stranger" and continued to the aspen grove behind the cabin to place the flowers on the grave. By midsummer, I was expecting another baby. Such a strange feeling to mourn the loss of a first child while preparing for the arrival of a second.

That autumn, fallen aspen leaves replaced my faded wildflowers, and by the time the first snowfall blanketed the grave, grief had loosened its grip on me. Baby Lukas arrived in the spring—safe and sound. As he changed from a helpless baby to inquisitive toddler, as quick as a blossom becomes a bean, I struggled with my fears which were compounded by Emil's job at the gold mine. He worked as a driller and assured me it was much safer than handling explosives, but I knew there was plenty of room for danger a thousand feet inside the earth.

Our son was now three years old and a bundle of words and energy, relishing his ability to try my patience. He shared a special bond with his father, tottering behind Emil like a puppy after a butterfly. While they frolicked, I worried. Was a bear skulking in the oak brush where Lukas played? Could a rattler be tucked below the boulder he scrambled over? The boy doubled down on his curiosity as I did my best to cover his bet with my motherly protection.

One day last week, after Emil brought our son back from the creek soaking wet, I overreacted imagining he'd fallen into a torrent and been carried downstream while his father was distracted panning for gold. Early on, I'd suggested we shouldn't place all our chips on what might be hidden beneath its waters, but he reminded me the wedding ring on my finger was proof the creek held the gold we needed for our future. Emil walked me down to the stream's edge to remind me how gently it rippled and explained that Lukas had gotten wet splashing after a minnow in a three-inch-deep puddle. Even so, my frustration bubbled to the surface.

"Maybe you should've been paying more attention to your son and less to your gold pan."

"Ah, Maggie, don't be mad at me. I was watching him, and he was safe."

"Aren't you tired of pulling worthless grit out of this creek?"

"That's the real reason you're irritated. Isn't it?"

I shrugged. "After five years, don't you think it's time for a change?"

"Soon, I promise." He pointed to the mountain above us. "The creek flows from up there where the gold veins are. Eventually, it shows up here."

"Eventually?"

"Don't fret. I still intend to give you the prettiest house in Lake City and the finest restaurant, too."

"It's not just the placer claim. I worry about you working in the mine."

"My job at the mine pays our bills, and I won't give up on the claim. Not yet." His tone was sharper than I expected, but I shrugged it off. Years of marriage had taught me which arguments were better left for another day.

I continued mulling over our conversation as I finished hoeing around the beans. Every so often, Emil found a nugget or two in the bottom of the pan—enough to motivate him to continue his quest. I likened him to the punters who once haunted my faro table at the saloon in Cripple Creek, winning just enough to keep them coming back. By now, we ought to have a bank vault full of gold nuggets to show for the effort. I leaned on the hoe and glanced across the valley to where my husband toiled in darkness. Then I admonished myself. I should trust him and remain patient.

All was quiet up at Mahala's place. I hadn't seen her since early this morning when she stopped by with a burlap sack in hand—ready to venture into the forest to hunt wild mushrooms. The old healer still enjoyed wandering the mountains when her rheumatism allowed.

"I'm hoping it's not too dry for chanterelles," she told me. "And with any luck, I'll find us some hawk's wing mushrooms. Lordy, do they make the best soup. Tasty enough to make you swoon."

In my mother hen frame of mind, I warned her not to wander far, reminding her, "Please be careful, Mahala, all kinds of critters lurk out there."

"Honey, after all my years upon this earth, I'm a might more anxious about the animals with two legs than those with four."

She had a point.

Judging by the sun's position above me, it was time I went inside to check on Lukas. I stepped over to the carrot row, my son's favorite vegetable, and set about collecting my bounty. I'd have a sizable batch to please him and enough to bake several carrot cakes to sell at the market in town. Baking cakes and pies added to our income and kept my cooking skills in play. It wasn't the same as making meals at my own restaurant, but good practice as I bided my time waiting for the placer claim to pay off.

As I closed the garden gate behind me, I spied Mahala making her way along the tree line above her cabin. Looked like she'd been successful in her mushroom hunt. Her burlap bag was full, and she was having difficulty managing it along with her cane. As I considered going to help, an animal hidden by the foliage moved behind her. Whatever the creature was, it paced with a purpose, stalking Mahala through the trees and scrub oak. Too sly to be a bear. As the animal crossed a gap in the pine trees, the sunlight revealed its form. A cougar. Mahala kept walking, oblivious to the danger. If I shouted a warning, the beast might try to pounce, leaving her no chance to escape.

I reached for the rifle leaning against the garden fence—as always surprised by its heft. The cougar had closed to within thirty feet of Mahala. No time to waste. I raised the rifle to my shoulder and aimed, then took a breath, exhaled, and fired. It was hard to tell who was more stunned by the gun's roar, me or the old healer. As the animal dropped to the ground, Mahala jerked around and saw me frozen in place at the garden gate staring at a spot behind her. She looked over her shoulder to the dead cougar and took a moment to consider what had just occurred. Then she turned back and nodded at me. This broke the spell I was under, and I lowered the rifle. It felt as heavy as a mine car full of ore.

She was standing over the cougar when I arrived. Its tongue lolled from its mouth, and blood flowed from the bullet wound down its cinnamon-colored neck. The rifle blast still drummed in my ears. Or was that my heart?

"Nice shot, honey," Mahala said as she prodded its paw with the tip of her cane. "He's a big 'un."

"A-are you all right?" I stammered. My hands shook as I held the gun over the beast, half-expecting it to rise and take revenge.

"Seems I should be asking you that question." She chuckled. "I don't believe Annie Oakley could've made a cleaner shot. He'd make a nice rug." Then she nodded. "Guess I should've listened to you this morning after all. If it weren't for you, that big 'ol cat would have feasted on this tough old bird, so thank you kindly."

"You're welcome," was all I could manage for a reply. It was beginning to sink in what I'd done. My insides jittered, threatening to leap up my throat and jump out.

"Come on now. Let's go see about the little 'un. The shot probably woke him up."

———————⋄⋄⋄⋄⋄———————

LATER, AS MAHALA and I sliced mushrooms for soup, Lukas sat at the table gnawing on a freshly picked carrot unaware of what had happened with the cougar. Much to our disbelief, he'd slept through the gunshot. I was excited for Emil to return from his shift to tell him about my big-game hunting adventure. He'd be glad to know I'd proven myself as the sure shot he'd hoped I'd be—if need be.

Outside, wheels scraping across rocks signaled someone approaching. When I peeked out the window, I saw two strangers dressed in miners' overalls in a wagon making its way up the hill. Emil's horse was tied to the back, but he wasn't with them.

I said under my breath, "Something's wrong."

Mahala hurried to my side.

"Papa's home." Lukas jumped down from the chair, laughing.

The wagon pulled to a stop in front of the cabin.

"I'll take care of the little 'un," Mahala offered as she walked him back to the table. "You go see."

I opened the door and pounded down the steps.

"Ma'am," said the driver. "Your husband was in an accident."

With one hand clutched to my throat and no breath in my lungs,

I stepped to the side of the wagon expecting to peer inside and see my worst fear realized. I nearly fainted when Emil sat up. He looked dazed, and the left side of his face was scraped and puffy, beginning to bruise.

"You're alive!"

"*Ja*, my love." His voice was thin and raspy.

"What happened?"

As the men jumped down from the wagon to help him, the driver said, "A section of rock he was drilling gave way and conked him on the noggin. We didn't think he should come home by himself. The old sawbones at the mine said he'll be fine in a day or two."

The men half-walked, half-carried Emil into the house where Lukas waited impatiently. When they laid him down on the bed, our son clung to his pant leg and said with a trembling voice, "Papa's sick."

"I'll be fine, little man. Bumped my head is all."

Mahala made him an onion and salt poultice for the swelling, and later that afternoon, he rose from the bed and stood before the mirror at the wash basin.

He gave me a crooked smile. "I believe I'm going to have a better shiner than the one I gave you."

"I think you're right," I said as I wrapped my arms around his waist. We gazed at each other in the glass. He smelled awful. "Phew, I may make you sleep outside tonight." We laughed, but I was still uneasy. "When I walked up to that wagon… I swear my heart stopped."

"I didn't mean to scare you, but accidents happen. I'll be all right."

"It wears me out, worrying about you."

"I should be the one concerned. You killed a cougar." He squeezed my hand. "Mahala told me. You saved her life, you know."

"I'm thankful both of your lives were spared today."

That evening before sunset, with Lukas tucked under his father's arm and both sleeping soundly, I hiked up the ridge with a large piece of canvas. The shock of the day's events pulsed through me, propelling me up to where the cougar had breathed its last. I wasn't sure how I'd get its body back down the mountain, but I was determined.

Dusk was quickening its approach as I spread out the cloth next to the cougar. The beast lay as still as the evening, stretched out on its side as if asleep. Poor dead thing. I grasped one of its paws and compared it to the size of my own hand. I had to stretch my fingers wide to match it. The pads were as smooth as river stones. I ran my fingertips over the beast's shoulder. Its body already stiffened by death. In an instant, I'd stilled this fierce animal's strength and power, but I'd saved my friend.

I tried not to look at its bloody wound as I lifted its front legs. Moving inches at a time, I placed the top half of it onto the canvas then stopped for a moment to rest. Next, I grabbed hold of the cougar's back legs and dragged its hindquarters onto the cloth. Then I wrestled the canvas under the body until it was centered. After draping each side of the cloth over the dead cat like a shroud, I lurched down the slope dragging it alongside me. Despite the animal's deadweight, I felt unburdened. Lukas and I could've lost our entire world, but fate had placed its bet on the wrong cards today, and the house had won. As I approached our cabin, now softly lit by the quarter moon above and a kerosene lantern within, I peered through the window.

In front of the fireplace was the perfect spot for the new rug I'd brought home.

—Pamela Redcliff was runner-up for the 2023 Women Writing the West LAURA Short Fiction Award. She has a bachelor's degree in Humanities (creative writing emphasis) and spent several years as a freelance writer, editor, and graphic designer. She also served as editor-in-chief of Star Wars Kids magazine, an international publication developed by Lucasfilm and Scholastic Books. For Troll Communications, she served as creative director and editor for several of their children's book titles. She currently lives on a farm in Ohio but was born and raised in Colorado with deep ancestral roots in New Mexico (of Jicarilla Apache and Hispanic lineage). Upon moving to Ohio, she took career detours into visual art then beekeeping and lavender

growing. She now has come full circle and returned to her first love, writing fiction. Living by the adage, "You can take the girl out of the West, but you can't take the West out of the girl," she returns to Western Colorado as often as possible to hike the desert canyons where she always finds inspiration.

Through Mud to Glory by W.H.D. Koerner

THROWAWAY

REGINA MCLEMORE

AS THE BIG man was finishing his second helping of biscuits and gravy, he caught a glimpse of someone staring in the window at him. It was that blasted Indian boy again!

Rising abruptly to his feet his sleeve caught the edge of the coffee pot and sent it and its contents flying. The pretty waitress flew to his side. "What happened, Marshal? Here, let me clean that up for you."

By the time she finished mopping the table and floor with a wet tea towel, the boy was long gone.

She gave him a big smile, batted her long eyelashes at him, and said, "Thank you kindly," when he told her to "keep the change" as he paid for his breakfast at Evansville's only café. She even patted him on the shoulder and said, "Come again" before he walked out the front door.

If he had been twenty years younger, he would have asked if she wanted to go to supper with him that evening. In the old days, he seldom passed up a chance to court a pretty woman. But, Marshal Emmett Palmer was nearing his sixtieth birthday, and today he was focused on finding the man that Judge Parker had sent him to arrest. With any luck, he would have Craig in handcuffs and on his way to Fort Smith before dark set in. He didn't like to be in unfamiliar territory after dark.

It put him at a disadvantage, and he needed every advantage he could get with Craig. Asa Craig had a reputation for having a fast hand and an even faster temper.

———————✦✦✦———————

AS HE MADE his way to where his horse was hitched, Emmett's luminous green eyes scanned the surrounding area. A Cherokee woman once told him that he had *wesa* eyes. He surprised her when he said, "You think I have cat eyes, huh?"

She laughed and said, "I didn't know you was Cherokee!"

"My granny was a full-blood, and she spoke the language. I remember some of it."

Then he pulled her so close that he could hear her pounding heart. "That's not all I remember."

She was the last woman he had let get close to him, and he didn't remember her name. It seems like it had bird in it somewhere. He had let her stay at the house for a few days, but by the end of the week, he couldn't stand to see her sleeping in Rose's bed anymore. On Saturday morning, he told her to get her things because he was taking her someplace. When he took her to Fort Smith, she looked around with scared eyes.

"Why did you bring me here?"

Emmett helped her down and handed her the bundle she had packed and several gold pieces.

"What's that for?"

"To buy you a train ticket to wherever you want to go. You can use what's left to help you start over in a new life."

She started to scream and push at him. "What makes you think I want a new life? I want *you!*"

He pushed her back. "I'm sorry, but I don't want you!"

The tears came then as she lowered herself to the ground, covering her head with her hands. "You brought me here to throw me away. You used me up, and now you're throwin' me away."

He tried to pry her hands away so he could see her eyes, but she fought him. Before he walked away, he said, "It's not your fault. There's something wrong with me. I can't love anybody since I lost my wife, but I hope you can find someone who will love you and treat you right."

———————

THAT HAD BEEN sixteen years ago—two years after his wife, Rose, had passed. He had been married to Rose for over twenty years and had no complaints about her. He was sure that she had plenty of complaints about him, but she seldom voiced any. He hoped she didn't know about the times he had strayed.

As he held Rose's hand when she was fading away from cancer, she had murmured, "I'm sorry, Emmett."

He patted her hand and said, "What did you do to feel sorry for?"

"I didn't give you a child to keep you company."

"Nobody except you can put up with me, and I have done plenty that I am sorry for."

"Funny. I don't remember any of that."

He had shed some tears then, and Rose, being Rose, tried to comfort him. She passed just a few hours later, smiling and looking out the window like she saw something pretty there. At her funeral, Preacher Brown had said, "I have no doubt whatsoever that Rose Palmer made Heaven."

———————

EMMETT SHOOK HIS head to clear his wandering mind and mounted his big bay horse. Right before he rode away the town sheriff caught his reins.

"That's a mighty big horse you have there, Marshal."

"He has to be big to carry me."

Taking in Emmett's six-foot plus frame, the sheriff nodded. "Yep, I can see that. I'm Tom Blevins. Mind if I ask what you're doin' in Sallisaw?"

"Here on Judge Parker's orders. Now, if you don't mind, daylight's a'burnin'."

Blevins didn't let go of the reins. "What kind of business?"

Emmett grimaced and turned a cold gaze on Blevins. "I'm not at liberty to say. Now get out of my way before I arrest you for interferin' with federal business."

Blevins took off his hat and waved him on his way. "Well, I don't want no trouble. Just tryin' to see if you needed any help."

"I will keep that in mind."

As he galloped away, Emmett noticed the Indian boy hiding behind a big oak, taking in his last conversation. Why had the sheriff acted so suspicious, and who was the boy who kept tailin' him?

A FEW MILES north of town he spotted the abandoned farm a jail trustee had described to him a few days ago. "It's where Asa lived as a boy, but when his folks moved away nobody ever tried to farm there. Asa knows the lay of the land so he uses it as a hideout. There's a cave nearby where he hides his loot and stuff he steals from folks."

"How do you know so much about him?"

"I used to ride with him two years ago. I quit him when he left me to die when I was wounded in a shootout with the law. They took me to be doctored and then threw me here in this blamed jail. If it hadn't been for listenin' to Asa, I would have been a free man today."

"You say he has a gang. How many?"

"Never more than two or three. He's too blamed hard to get along with and will cheat you if he gets half a chance. Though that probably ain't so easy to do now since he hooked up with the law."

"What do you mean?"

"Well, it's just a rumor, but there's some that say some lawman is watchin' out for Asa and warns him off if anybody's gettin' too close."

HOPING THAT NO lawman had notified Asa of his approach, Emmett hid his horse in the woods and approached the farmhouse on foot. Six-shooter in hand, he crept up to a window. Three bearded men played poker at a wooden kitchen table. One of them jumped up and yelled, "You're cheatin' again, Asa!"

The man Emmett assumed was Asa grabbed the smaller man by the arm and jerked him back in his chair. "Shut your mouth, Frank, and sit down! You're too stupid to know the difference between cheatin' and playin' smart."

Frank scrambled from his chair and ran from the kitchen. Asa stood up, drew his Colt, and shot him in the back of the head. Frank slumped to the floor.

Asa's surviving partner wiped the sweat from his brow. "Why did you do that for?"

"Calm down. Jim. Just one less man to share the loot with. Now drag him out in the woods so he won't stink the house up."

Jim walked over to Frank's corpse, then turned around and looked back at Asa.

"What are you waitin' for?"

"Thought you might help me."

"Well, you thought wrong. Now get rid of him, *pronto.*"

Grumbling under his breath, Jim pulled the body through the back door. Unseen and unmoving, Emmett waited in the woods.

When Jim got within reach, he brought his revolver down on the back of his head, knocking him out. Emmett gagged Jim, bound him to a big oak, and dragged the corpse out of sight. Only one to go.

He was creeping back to the cabin when he heard hoofbeats and a familiar voice yell out, "Asa, are you there?"

It was Sheriff Blevins—warning Asa about Emmett. Now, the odds were against him again. He needed to get some distance between himself and the cabin and make another plan.

Then he heard a low whisper. "Marshal?"

He turned to see the familiar form of the Indian boy standing by his horse.

"What in tarnation are you doin' here, boy? Don't you know you could get killed just by bein' here?"

"I came to help you."

"I don't remember askin' for your help."

Emmett did a quick scan of the woods. "How did you get here anyway?"

"I stole a horse and followed you. I tied him up back in the woods. I don't have a gun, but I got a knife, and I'm good at throwin' it."

"Knives generally don't stand up to fast guns. You need to get on your horse and ride away, boy."

"I come to help."

Emmett shoved him to the ground. "I don't want your help! Now, git, before you get yourself killed."

The boy picked himself up and glared at Emmett. "All right! Have it your way. I'm gone."

Emmett watched until the boy was out of sight. He had only ridden a few yards when a shot rang out. His horse stumbled and fell to the ground. Emmett managed to get out from under him and had just gotten to his feet when he heard voices coming through the woods.

"Good shot, Blevins. Marshal, stay right where you are if you value your life."

Emmett shut his eyes, gathering his thoughts. "You know Judge Parker knows about your involvement with Craig, Sheriff. He will be sending more marshals if I don't make it back."

Blevins smirked. "I believe you're lyin', Marshal. If Parker knew anything, he would have had you arrest me first to keep word from gettin' to Craig."

"Well, how do you explain the fact I knew exactly where Craig was?"

Blevins scratched his head. "Well, now that does puzzle me, Marshal, but it don't really matter because we're moving all our ill-gotten gains tonight. Right, Craig?"

Craig sighed. "Much as I hate to leave this old place, you're right. Now, shoot the marshal and help me load the stuff in a wagon."

"Sorry, Craig, but my deputies are going to be expectin' me back anytime. If I don't go back to town, they will come lookin' for me. Since Jim seems to have hightailed it, why don't you make the marshal load the loot in the wagon, and then you can shoot him? I'll meet you at Cookson tonight at the usual place, and we'll hole-up until it's safe to travel."

Craig let out a string of curse words. "Do you see how big that marshal is? If he ever gets a hold of me, there will be no fight to it. He can crush me with one hand."

Blevins laughed until he almost lost his breath.

Insulted, Craig waved his Colt at him. "Don't you be laughin' at me!"

"Aww, I'm sorry, Craig. Just hard to believe you're scared of an old, used-up law man. All you gotta do is keep your gun trained on him and keep your distance. If he gives you any trouble, shoot him in the toe or something, just enough to wound him. Just don't hurt him enough so he can't be your pack mule. I'll drive the wagon over to the cave, and then I'll head out. You both can ride with me. Just remember to keep your gun on the marshal."

A few minutes later, they arrived at the cave, and Blevins untied his horse from the back of the wagon and rode off. As he rode away, he said, "Nothin' personal, Marshal. You just were in the wrong place at the wrong time. See you tonight, Craig."

Emmett yelled out, "Wait just a minute, Sheriff. Since you are bein' so nice to me, I want to offer you a word of advice."

Blevins chuckled. "All right. Go ahead."

"Craig has already killed one partner tonight What's to keep him from killin' you and takin' it all?"

"Nothin' much, except I'm smarter than him and a much better shot.'

Emmett ducked as a bullet whizzed past his head. "Get to walkin', Marshal, or the next one will leave a mark."

Craig walked a few feet behind him holding a lantern. "Remember I'm right behind you, and I got the light and the gun. Don't try anything stupid."

"If I try anything, it won't be stupid."

"Just shut up and keep walkin'."

When Emmett got to the stacks of gold coins and miscellaneous items, he looked around for a weapon. He saw a pair of golden candlesticks near the back of the pile, but Craig was watching him too closely for him to get near them.'

"There's some empty bags layin' near the gold. Fill them up with gold and carry them out first."

"You aren't helpin'?"

"I can't take my eye off of you long enough to lift somethin'. Now, do what I say, right now!"

"All right. All right."

Emmett, heavily laden with four bags of gold, walked back to the wagon,. Craig, following close behind him, yelled, "Toss the bags in as far as you can throw them."

He threw three in and, intentionally, dropped the fourth.

"You clumsy fool! Pick that up and throw it in."

At the same time Emmett picked up the bag of gold to throw at Craig, he looked up to see him struggling to get a knife out of the side of his neck. Emmett lunged and threw himself onto the wounded criminal.

Craig offered little resistance as Emmett drew the knife from his neck. "Give me your shirt, boy. I need to stop the bleedin'."

"Why?"

"Because I've sworn to protect all lives, even those of people who deserve to die."

The boy sighed, took off his shirt, and handed it to Emmett. "Is he goin' to live?"

The marshal tore the thin shirt into strips and packed the wound. "Hard to say. It don't look good, though. He's already passed out from losin' blood. I'll load him in the wagon, and you can follow me to Fort Smith on your stolen horse. We'll get everything sorted out with Judge Parker. He should go easy on you since you just stole it to help me."

The boy frowned. "I was plannin' on keepin' him. I ain't never had a horse of my own."

"We'll talk about it when we get to Fort Smith."

"All right. I have some other things I need to talk to you about."

"Guess I owe you that much. You can come bunk at my place tonight after we talk to Judge Parker."

It was almost seven o'clock by the time they had finished their business at the courthouse. The judge loaned them fresh horses and said they could ride them until Emmett found replacements.

"Mister Marshal, I was wonderin'. What's to keep that crooked sheriff from comin' back to get what was left in the cave?"

"The judge sent Bass Reeves and Heck Thomas after him, so they'll catch him wherever he goes."

"Can we talk now?"

"Can it wait until breakfast? I'm awfully tired."

"It's waited this long, so I guess it can wait a little longer."

Late the next morning, after the boy finally got filled-up, Emmett poured them both a cup of coffee and led him to the front porch. "Sit there on that bench. We can talk here. Now what's on your mind? Why have you been followin' me all week?"

"My mother told me to find you."

"Who's your mother?"

"Mary Redbird."

"Do I know her?"

"You *knew* her. She's dead now."

"Can't say I remember her, but I have met a lot of people over the years. What is your name?"

"Emmett Redbird."

A sense of dread filled the marshal, but he held it down. "Funny we have the same first name."

"Not so funny. I was named after my father."

The boy stood up, and Emmett took a good look at him. He was tall for a Cherokee, maybe an inch shy of six feet, but his most outstanding characteristic was his eyes. They were bright green, wesa eyes. Emmett took a big breath and slowly let it out. "Now listen, boy, I like you, but despite what you believe, you can't be my son."

The boy took a big swallow of his coffee. "My mom said you would say that, and she told me what to say when you did."

The hand that held Emmett's coffee trembled. "And what's that?"

"She said to tell you that God might forgive you for throwing her away, but He won't forgive you if you throw away your son."

Emmett took out his big white handkerchief, wiped his eyes, and blew his nose. "Well, your ma might have made a mistake sendin' you to me, but I'm willin' to give it a shot if you are."

"*Wado*, Father."

"I can't remember it in Cherokee, but you're welcome."

—Like many Oklahoma Cherokees, Regina Philpott McLemore's ancestors walked the Trail of Tears. They arrived in Indian Territory in February of 1839 and settled less than 20 miles from where she lives now. Her historical fiction series, Cherokee Passages, relates stories they might have told about the Trail and their lives in Indian Territory.

The love of stories, books, and history has always influenced McLemore's life. Beginning in 2011, her work has appeared in several publications, and she is a columnist for Saddlebag Dispatches. *Her first historical fiction novel,* Cherokee Clay, *which received a Will Rogers Medallion award, was published in 2020.* Cherokee Stone *was released in 2021, followed by* Cherokee Steel *in 2022.*

Being a citizen of the Cherokee Nation and a student of its history and culture, McLemore is listed as a consultant on the Cherokee Film site. She recently served as a script advisor on the Hallmark movie, Love in the Great Smoky Mountains. *Currently, she is working on* The Adventures of Cherokee Wesa, *a middle-grade children's book. In her leisure time, she enjoys volunteering, traveling, visiting relatives, shopping, and spending time with her husband and pets.*

BAD RIVER

RICK SAPP

SOME OF WHAT you will read is true.

Don't imagine that I know all the details. I do not.

Even after these many years though, everybody I meet claims they were present that Saturday night. The night they arrested Robbie Calkins and his horse. The night the law threatened the cowboys with jail and fines they couldn't possibly pay. It was, after all, the kind of sultry summer evening that made crickets fall silent and reach for their church fan. And alcohol was involved, and women.

The bars closed early in Pierre, South Dakota, and every poor soul who could still walk or drive galloped across the Missouri River to Fort Pierre, and especially to The Silver Spur Saloon. There, music still jangled and bartenders still poured, and gals held on to their smiles for a couple more hours. But I get ahead—

Steve Nelson introduced me. Said I could probably hunt at Robbie's place southwest of the Grasslands, long as I didn't act too much the know-it-all writer. He figured Robbie would be fine with my bow and arrows. He would be curious to see if I could sneak up close to a pronghorn antelope, and Steve offered to drive.

A buffalo stampede on that gravel road would have raised less dust than Steve's truck. He pulled up at Robbie's lopsided mailbox and yanked out a fist-full of bills and flyers and free newspapers.

"Ought to straighten his post," he said.

Steve held the cracked four-by-four upright while I stomped dirt and rocks around it to keep it standing. Even then, it leaned somewhat to starboard, so Steve re-tied the yellow nylon rope holding the mailbox on top, and we stepped back to admire our work. The door, swinging by one rusty hinge, resisted closing until Steve fastened it with a stick of Spearmint chewing gum. The red "we-got-mail" flag lay broken in the ditch. We left it right there.

"Won't stay up long out here. Robbie's not much on mail," Steve said. "The Post Office refused to deliver after the box fell off, but Robbie wouldn't put it back up. Told 'em he didn't want their damn mail anyhow. So, they tossed his correspondence into a General Delivery box for a couple months until the co-op threatened to cut off his electricity for not paying his bills."

"Looks kind of run down," I said, offering an outsider's view of the house and grounds.

Steve hunched over the wheel of his truck. "Robbie's lonely. Got no incentive to fix anything since his wife left."

"When was that?"

"Maybe eight, ten years ago. It's hard to find a woman who'll put up with the hard work and long hours of a ranch. Mostly though, with women, it's the isolation."

Robbie's home, as I discovered, was less a house than a frontier ruin kept standing with black coffee and brandy at sunup and whiskey neat—or beer if there was no whiskey—after sundown. Between those fermented spirits Robbie moped restlessly around what he called his spread.

Steve handed Robbie the fistful of mail, and the cowboy tossed everything across the kitchen counter, upsetting a cat sunning itself in the window. "Have a seat," he said. "I'll put the coffee on." He offered us Spam sandwiches with mayonnaise, but we said we'd already eaten.

I kept my mouth shut while Steve and Robbie talked dry spells and beef prices and cussed the government, and Robbie said it would be fine to stay awhile. I could bunk in the spare room.

The next morning, Robbie said he'd show me a couple places I might could hunt up an antelope. His spread was big country, scarred by a thoughtless, wandering stream and bewildering gullies that crossed and recrossed the mixed-grass prairie. Not a tree in sight. It was beautiful.

"Don't get lost and you'll be okay," Robbie said.

"What if I get lost?"

"I'll watch for circlin' buzzards. They always spot dead meat." It sounded thoughtful but not funny, and he kind of snickered. "Or you could fire three arrows in the air." An old joke.

Robbie halted the truck. "Get out and lift that calf there into the back. I need to dose her." I just stared. A sickly looking brown animal stared back, its glassy eyes seeming to focus nowhere in particular.

Robbie laughed. He picked up the sick calf as easy as if he was sliding a chair across the kitchen linoleum and placed it gently in the back of the chugging pickup. There it lay down and snuggled into the mess of straw, empty oil cans, fast food wrappers, and unidentifiable pieces of equipment.

"Nothin' to it," Robbie grinned. He was all of a proud jaw, a rumpled John Deere tractor hat that set crooked on top of his thatch of sandy hair, and solid eighty-proof muscle.

"We'll go spotlight some jacks tonight," he said.

Night was cool as a sulky mare, and the sky such a black as is rarely observed in luminous societies. Constellations winked brilliantly overhead. Galaxies so distant their light departed millions of years ago merged with planets and satellites, and Robbie's spread hosted this display every night, unmarred by one single human light source—interrupted only by the occasional downward-dog barometer.

I'd have been happy to lie on my back, nestle into the hay in which the calf had bedded down, and stare into the abyss. Robbie wasn't having that.

"Climb up," he said. "I'll shine the spot, and when you see a jack, you take a shot."

I hiked up into the bed of the pickup with my bow and Robbie revved the old Ford. I inferred we were hunting jack rabbits, which scrambled plentifully, but warily, through the sagebrush and cactus. When the time came to draw the bow and loose an arrow though, Robbie couldn't drive straight, and I couldn't shoot straight, and the rabbits ignored us and hopped away.

Then, not one to let an opportunity to shine pass, I fell out of the truck and landed on my head. Robbie had motored us into a prairie dog town and immediately the ride reminded me of The Zipper at the State Fair. People say you see stars when you bang your head like that, but all I remember is Robbie's grizzled face and tobacco-stained teeth when he picked me up like the calf and tossed me into the bed of the truck.

"You could at least put me up front," I complained.

"One drunk in front is plenty," he said. "Two drunks and we'd run off a cliff and get killed. 'Sides, we got to get goin' and I imagine that bump on the head is gonna cause you to blow, so you're welcome."

Next morning, way before I was ready, Robbie shook my shoulder. "Get up. Let's go."

A whisper of gray light outlined the grassland hills, but the trailer, complete with two horses and their tack, was already hitched to the back of the asthmatic pickup.

"Coffee." Robbie pointed to a mug on the dash. The handle was broken and I doubted it had ever been washed. With only one resident in the house, what was the point?

"How's your head?"

"It's okay," I lied. Actually, it throbbed, my shoulder ached, and my back felt like a cracked two-by-four.

"You ride don't ya?"

"A horse?"

Robbie looked at me like I stepped out of a spaceship. "We're goin' to race, son. Heard of the Bad River Suicide Ride?"

Something in the way he asked should have warned me, made me get out of the truck, and go back to bed. Instead, I allowed how I didn't know what he was talking about.

"It's simple," he said. "A bunch of city fellers thought they'd bring customers into town if they could put on a kind of spectacular cowboy thing. They'd make some money and all the local dum-dums with horses—dum-dums like us—would have some fun. The object is to gallop up a steep hill. The fastest horse wins. Like I said, it's simple."

"That's it? What are the rules?"

"What rules?"

"Well," I considered, "like a men's class and a women's class. Or stallions versus mares or," I racked my brains for what little I knew about horses because I knew nothing at all about horse racing, "Arabians say versus... whatever."

Robbie squinted at me in a peculiar manner, and I could tell, even in the glare of green light from the dash, that he thought I was an ignorant yahoo. He floored the pickup to get going over the ditch and bounced a hard left onto the gravel road. That spilled hot coffee and set me to howling like a scalded coyote. He thought it was funny.

"Rules? And women? Don't no women do The Ride. They got more sense. And ain't no rules either. Best advice—try not to get yourself killed. And hope your horse don't get busted-up neither. That's the rules."

"Why didn't they just put on a rodeo?"

"Hell, everybody does that. We already got two or three. This little gallop though, it's something different."

And it was.

The day unfolded fast. "You gonna ride? Give it a shot?"

"Seriously?" I looked up at that hill. Looked straight up to the top where a bunch of little fellows about the size of ants were sticking flags in the ground. "You're kidding, right?"

Robbie didn't make it to the top that day and neither did his horses. That's about all I recall.

Steve told me later that it was an interesting day even though nobody got killed. But I still had a headache and a swelling the size of Mount Rushmore on the sides and the top and the other side of my head.

"It's your own fault," Robbie said. "Stead of jumping out of the truck head first you oughta been shootin' that bow. Else pick a softer spot to land. What kind of fool gonna jump out of a moving pickup head first, anyway?"

After the fall, he had dosed me with a democratic excess of eighty-proof tonic and the pain subsided for a minute. I ascribed my blurry vision and the nest of bees in my ears to his medication.

I remember that the ambulances stayed busy that morning. A couple large animal veterinarians scrambled around all day cussing cowboys, and several hippie animal rights activists got their butts whipped with their own protest signs. Me? I spent most of the day sleeping in a pile of hay which I eventually discovered was compounded with a liberal dose of horse apples.

And then there was Robbie's cattle dog, an ornery Blue Heeler named Butt Head, that rode in the front seat of the pickup. On race day it seemed to think lifting his leg on my boots while I slept was a capital idea. So all in all, it was a pretty nice day.

The Ride was sure enough interesting if you like to watch men and horses thrash around in the dirt on the side of a mountain and come down cussing and spitting... and the horses could cuss and complain better than the cowboys.

By late afternoon, my vision began to clear and the cowboys were most plumb give out—the ones that could still stand up without assistance. Robbie brought his horses back to the trailer, looked me over, and told me I was "sure enough a-idjit" for laying down in horse poo and letting his dog pee on my boots. I had to get myself cleaned up. We were going dancing, he said.

The Ride wasn't the day's main event.

The main event started nowhere near the Bad River.

Pierre may be the capital of South Dakota, but its general respectability is still plodding west with the covered wagons. Dignity will catch its citizens by surprise one day and lead the town to ruin, but when I was present for The Ride, it was still a town of deer skinning, duck plucking, occasional turkey or elk calling, and two-stepping in dance halls shunned by the town's reputable folk—lawyers, preachers, and old maid teachers.

The night of The Ride, every cowboy who could walk, and some who couldn't, were hungry and thirsty—mostly thirsty—although the smart fellows had quietly begun to tonic their thirst before they made the dash for the top of that impossible hill. The devil of it was that the vilest horse wrangler, the man with Bad River dirt smashed into his hair and vomit on his shirt and horse poo on his boots, his Stetson rimmed with sweat, and maybe with a bandage or two, had it made that night. The ladies of South Dakota turned out and the cowboys turned on.

"You dance, honey?"

"Who, me?"

A pretty little size twenty brunette in an outfit with spangles and a universe of stars on her shiny black snip-toe boots stared up at me. Her face gleamed like a full moon over a duck blind, and I noticed Robbie pointing to the dance floor. He was assisting a peroxide blonde with her intoxication and seemed comfortably, thoroughly contented.

"I don't know. You'll have to guide me through it."

She did, although I stumbled around the floor like a walrus. About the time I was getting the hang of it, with music screeching so loud you could see the singer's tonsils wiggle, that little filly smiled and said, all very sweet and polite, "Excuse me for a moment, please."

It could have been a misunderstanding, a simple miscommunication, but I saw her a bit later swinging like a gazelle, a nymph, a fairy goddess in the arms of an elderly cowboy who must have left the graveyard just for this one night. She pointed at me, and the old man kind of snickered. That didn't seem real polite, and pretty soon, my head started to hurt again, so I went out and fell asleep beside Butt Head in Robbie's pickup.

"Move over, big boy."

It was the peroxide blonde, squeezing me between Butt Head and her amplified proportions. The dog gave a low growl and showed me his teeth. I asked Robbie why he brought the dog to The Ride and he said, "He gets lonely out there on the spread, and it's his opportunity to do a little socializing. Plus, anybody gets too near my truck—well, he's a mite territorial."

Formerly—just minutes before—the truck smelled strongly of motor oil and chewing tobacco, wet dog and manure. Now, that sweet, manly odor was sideswiped by the latest perfume sale at the Walmart.

Robbie gunned the truck out on Highway 14 and made fast for the river.

"I'm Randi, with an 'i.' What's your name?"

I told her and immediately thought of Miss Size Twenty inside the saloon. Randi with an "i" followed up, "What do you do? Do you work for Robbie?"

I answered that question, too.

"Oh, like Hemingway." And my ego blew up a couple notches.

"Why weren't you out dancing? There's lots of pretty girls would love to swing you around." About that time Robbie pulled into The Silver Spur Saloon in Fort Pierre.

Inside, the Mountain Time Silver Spur was just like the Central Time place we'd just closed, only more so. A steaming overload of country heartbreak and whirling, sweating bodies. Overhead fans swirled thick cigarette smoke, drunks tried to drown in the spilled beer, and people screamed just to be heard over the fiddle and guitar.

I found Steve already at the bar and ordered a beer. There on the dance floor was Miss Size Twenty swiveling around her undead partner like a petite Moses parting the waters of the Red Sea. She caught me looking at her and smiled.

We didn't talk much, Steve and I, except for a casual comment about the ladies, all of whom avoided us as if we were lepers—apparently word was out that we couldn't dance a lick. I didn't pay a whole lot of attention to the goings on because my head was pounding again, and I figured I only had to endure a couple more hours before we hit the trail, you might say, for home.

Consequently, I missed the fracas. I say fracas because by the time I got turned around and focused on the action Robbie grabbed me by the arm.

"Come on, fancy man. We got some business," he said and he jerked me away from the bar with one of those fists that could pick up a calf and a look on his face that clearly said, don't mess with me nohow.

I had no idea what I'd done. I hadn't made a pass at Robbie's peroxide blonde or said anything unsettling about Waylon Jennings or Travis Tritt being soft in the socket.

Robbie headed for the door, and in his grasp, I did a creditable imitation of a rodeo clown. Half a dozen cowboys pushed their way to the entrance with us. They appeared, best I could tell, being jerked unceremoniously through the crowd, altogether pissed off.

"What's wrong? What did I do?"

"Ain't about you." Robbie spat on the parking lot and let go of my arm. "That son of a bitch called me a farmer. We're going to show him the difference between a cattleman and a farmer."

And so it began.

In the half-light of The Spur's neon beer signs and a flickering street lamp, Robbie backed his horses out of the trailer and squared them away with saddles, bridles, and all the paraphernalia for a ride. Only problem in my eyes was he had two horses, and it was one o'clock a.m. and all the cowboys were splashed.

"Mount up."

"Me?"

"Climb up there. I'm gonna teach you how to dance."

I knew which side of the horse to get on, to hold the reins in one hand, and the horn in the other. Beyond that, I'd just watch Robbie. Do exactly what he did. That was my first mistake.

Steve stood outside in the milling crowd and watched the cowboys mount up. He came over while the cowboys talked among themselves. The horses were nervous and the crowd anxious to see what was about to happen. "You sure you want to do this?"

"Do what?" I asked, but right then the cowboys started moving toward the batwing doors of The Spur. My horse put its nose in the tail of Robbie's animal and carried me right along with everybody else.

"You watch out up there!" I heard one of the cowboys yell, "These farmers is coming through."

Then up we all galloped right up the steps, across the porch, and into the very inner sanctum of that dance hall. Well, I'd never heard such a commotion of women screaming and men cussing, and the band barely tapering off until those farmers were inside wrecking tables and overturning chairs. Men jumped over the bar and women ran for the Ladies Room.

Robbie shouted, "Keep that music going. We want to two-step." Those ranchers and their horses began circling the dance floor and somebody shouted, "Where's that dude what called us farmers? Wherever you hiding at, get out here and get your butt whipped!"

Out of the corner of my eye, I saw Randi with an "i" wilt into a corner and disappear about the time the bartender jumped up and shouted that he had a shotgun and was, "calling the cops."

The farmers either didn't hear him or didn't care because the band took up "Dancin' Cowboys" by the Bellamy Brothers and the place sort of went wild. The farmers pulled gals up behind them on their horses, and folks kicked the broken furniture aside and handed them cans of Coors beer. Even handed me one, and then that Size Twenty brunette smiled up at me, and I had to do the right thing, of course, and give her a hand on board, but when I tried to lift her up, she pulled me right off and with one foot still in the stirrup I went around that dance floor twice.

It was mayhem inside The Spur. Flash bulbs going off left and right. Cowboys screaming at the top of their lungs… and right about then we heard sirens. Before we could get outside, there were cops of every size and quality, even a Canadian Mountie, shoving folks out the doors. All the patrons except we farmers, and unfortunately just at this time, I had scrambled back into the saddle and was looking around for Size Twenty when a cop caught my bridle.

"Where you going, son? You climb on down now, you hear?"

The jail wasn't exactly a Holiday Inn, but everyone got bailed out the next day, even me. Because the whoopee had caused so much media commotion, Pierre and Fort Pierre were suddenly in national headlines. And that's rare.

The judge seemed to think it was funny, busting up The Spur. Said he wished he'd been there. He didn't say he wished he'd been there to ride alongside those farmers, just that—like everybody else in the capital the next week—he'd have liked to have seen it so he could tell his grandkids he was present that night. The night the cowboys danced with their horses in The Silver Spur.

It helped that a lot of local folks who had been gyrating in The Spur that night were present when the bailiff trooped us into court. The judge knew all the cowboys and called them by name, but when he got to me he asked, "Who are you and how did you get mixed up in this? You some kind of troublemaker?"

That's when Randi with an "i" raised up from the audience and shouted, "He's a writer, judge. Like Hemingway."

"Ahh. So you're the one in the photograph," the judge said. "Not from around here, I see."

He picked up a copy of *The Capital Journal* and there I was, clear as all get-out, leaning down to lift Size Twenty up onto Robbie's spare horse.

Well, His Honorableness levied fines and parceled out the damages. Because nobody got hurt too bad and the man who called Robbie a farmer came in to court and sort of apologized, we all went home. Later that week, after a veterinarian certified that none of them were injured, the sheriff released the horses.

The next day I said goodbye to Robbie. He pounded me on the back, pulled off his John Deere cap, and mashed it down on my head. "Don't never let nobody tell you you can't dance, cowboy."

He called me a cowboy.

THESE DAYS I remember my brief cowboy experience with pride.

"Is there any more coffee?"

"Of course, darlin'. You keep right on working. I'll bring it to you."

My heavenly Size Twenty skitters through our kitchen door, a bit sideways because she's growing a wee cowboy now. I tip up my John Deere hat and give her a smooch as she pours.

"Did I ever tell you how grateful I am that you bailed me out?" I pat her stomach. "Boy or girl, we ought to name our baby Robbie. What do you think?"

"My Hemingway."

For luck, we reach up and touch that framed newspaper picture of us holding hands in The Spur. Size Twenty on her tiptoes, the stars on her boots flashing bright as a prairie moon, and me about to fall face-first on that dance hall floor.

—*Freelance writer Rick Sapp describes his life as "an adventure a day." He earned college degrees in anthropology and political science and served in the U.S. Army. He is especially fond of memories from years in Colorado and New Mexico, but has also lived in Germany and France, and has hiked with a tent and sleeping bag on every continent except Antarctica. Thus, at any time of day, he may slip into a confused mixture of Spanish, German or French. Rick says he has been privileged to write about a wide variety of subjects—hunting in Africa, sailing in the Virgin Islands, urban planning, individual biographies—fiction and nonfiction. He now teaches outdoor skills as well as creative writing at Young Harris College in North Georgia—the Institute for Continuing Education—where his black Stetson and trail-worn, square-toed boots have become his calling card. Rick is married to a musician and chef, has two grown children and two vivacious Australian shepherd dogs.*

WILLIAM LETSKY'S FUNERAL

DEAN HALLIDAY SMITH

"YOU GONNA BET that cigar you've been mushing up, Billy?" I asked William Letsky after wrinkling my nose at what he was doing to his unlit cigar.

William "Wild Bill" Letsky rat-grinned at me across the green felt of the poker table. The light from the Gold Shoe's ceiling lamps cast bizarre shadows on his jaw and neck. Saloon noise rolled over us. The portly Angelo's piano plinking mixed with raucous whoops and laughter from nearby tables.

"Starin' at them cards won't turn those horse apples into aces," Stump Barber said to Letsky from across the table. He gave his bulbous, veined nose a rough swipe. "Did you pick up that starin' business from a Chinese poohbah, Buffalo Billy?"

"Don't go changing his name, Stump," I warned. "Might change his luck."

Stump grunted.

"Well, hey, Wild Bill, it's hot as blazes in here," Wilbur Parsons said as he fanned away from the other side of the table. "Do we gotta wait for January before you bet?"

Letsky thumbed his cards apart with a practiced disinterest. His ruddy face and neck bore pock marks—maybe smallpox as a child. Letsky liked my nickname for him, but he wouldn't know the business end of Wild Bill Hickock's pistol from a wooden pitchfork. A meek lawyer, Letsky rarely raised his voice and seemed half asleep much of the time during his court cases. He wore his long hair ragged with curls like Hickock, but all neatness ended with any absent-minded run of his hand on his head.

Inside the saloon, everyone lent a hand in stirring the stifling spring air against the relentless heat. Evenings tended to cool down outside, but not inside saloons where poker tables, cigars, and whiskey were being used and consumed. Hand-held fans were flapping at full speed. The tables were full of gamblers, table-watchers, whores, and the usual tipsy piffle artists begging for another free drink from bartenders.

Cigar smoke filled the saloon. My first whiff of tobacco had come in a North Carolina tobacco barn late in the war. Two thousand of our Iowa brigade were helping ourselves to well-cured leaves for rolling our own cigars. Sherman had ordered us to burn everything. We were obeying him. We were taking our time. Our pious dumb Brigadier, William Belknap, rode up and barked while the gol-dang Rebs were still out there, "Torch the gol-dang tobacco barn, and git your gol-dang asses back in the war!" Belknap galloped away, his aides trying to keep up like hounds on a raccoon.

I said, "Wilbur, I don't think Wild Bill is stupid, but Doc Ackerman says he might have something that is catching."

Wilbur snorted.

"Shut it up, Davenport." Letsky shot me and Wilbur a surly look prompting more hoots and a big grin from Wilbur.

"Billy, Davenport has won the last three hands. He probably has you beat agin."

Letsky slowly shook his head. "I'm letting the great lawyer, Silas Davenport, dangle a bit afore I take his money."

"Kind of you," I said.

Letsky dragged his sleeve over sweat beads annoying his forehead. He nervously rolled his small cigar back and forth from one corner of his mouth to the other. He thought rolling unlighted cigars made him look like a seasoned poker player. Between rolls, he caught the cigar in his front teeth and bounced the captured part up and down in his mouth like a water dowser seeking hidden moisture.

Earlier, I had watched from the back bench while Letsky won a case in Judge Elmo Powell's court. Letsky's client owed money to a hardware store in Offerle, but a witness for the plaintiff testified while drunk. Letsky's client disputed the debt and the man's wife claimed the title of County Temperance Queen. Powell didn't want temperance zealots after him at election time, and as a drunk's testimony is inherently unreliable, Powell awarded judgment to Letsky's client. Letsky had already spent part of his fee at our table.

The cigar began its bumping and grinding dance again.

I leaned my chair back against the wall behind me. Sahra, a buxom brunette, leaned her splendid posterior against the wall next to me. I had the most cash in front of me so she figured I might want to spend it with her. She leaned onto my shoulder, curious to discover if the breast she purposefully pressed against my ear, imbued with the essence of Lily of the Valley, might arouse something.

Sahra's power could ensnare the affections of any gentleman. Letsky glanced at Sahra's breasts, and his face turned red when he saw that I saw him looking. Wild Bill's knowledge of women equaled his knowledge of Hickock's gun. Sahra's breast in Letsky's ear would melt his teeth.

I, however, bent forward and kissed the closest breast, earning a playful swat from Sahra. No freebies here. Every touch had a price. She leaned in, pressing against me, her voice a sultry whisper promising a night with her would make every cowboy from here to the Cherokee Outlet green with envy. I'd have difficulty standing in the morning, let alone moving. Sahra was a true temptress and supposedly, her word was as good as gold. But my three tens stared at a thirty-dollar pot. Truth be, I wanted those thirty bucks more than I wanted her. When I play poker, even Moses carrying his stone tablets through the saloon door couldn't get my attention.

Sahra gave up and moseyed past Billy, gently caressing his cheek, and proceeded to give us an attractive hip banging show as she took her Lily of the Valley in a slow-walk past the rest of the saloon's tables to the bar. Letsky's head and eyes followed.

"Go on, Billy," Wilbur teased. "Take your filly upstairs. We'll save your spot."

Letsky turned back quickly, his face flushed. His cigar began its nervous hopping again. Wilbur laughed, shaking his head.

The Gold Shoe's tables were full. The saloon's strict conduct code helped. The Shoe's simple and absolute rules kept poker, whiskey, and pistols apart.

A hulking figure named Harb Dubois held court at the far end of the long bar ensuring strict enforcement of the saloon's no-gun rule. His bald head sported a few stubborn hairs, and three jagged scars marred his tough face, like he'd tussled with a bear and lived to tell it. Over Letsky's shoulder, I watched Dubois deal with a couple of railroad switchmen looking to join a game. He cracked open their pistols. The rounds clinked onto the bar. Dubois swept the bullets into a whiskey glass keeping them as collateral. The switchmen got their empty guns back, along with the privilege to order drinks. Harb warned in no uncertain terms, if they caused any trouble or reloaded their pistols, his ax handle would break a bone they held dear.

Letsky finally bet five dollars. Everyone at the table folded but me. I bent over, thumbing my stack of coins and peering at him like I would raise him. No sense getting greedy. I tossed five silver dollars onto the big pot.

"I call. Show us them puny things, Wild Bill."

Letsky spread his pairs of eights and threes on the pot. He rocked back in his chair grinning, almost bumping into a large man standing behind him.

Hunk Paprete, a brawny and constantly unemployed half-breed buffalo skinner, eyed the table over Letsky's shoulder. Paprete's noxious stink reached me. A mix of the rotgut he swilled and the awful puking coming afterwards.

"You ain't gonna like them cards, Davenport," Letsky said, pointing.

I laid down my three tens.

Paprete's free hand snatched Wild Bill's hair and pulled back hard. Letsky managed an "Aaggg," before Paprete's skinning knife swiftly sliced Letsky's throat open. The blood sprayed like a dark secret laid bare—splattering the table and the triple tens I had laid down over the chips. Letsky tried to scream, but he had been cut forever silent. His wide desperate eyes fixed me to my seat like a butterfly pinned to a display board. He clutched his throat trying to keep the blood inside. He tried to stand, but he toppled forward colliding with the edge of the table. Coins and cards jumped into the air then fell back on the table. He bounced once and fell back into the chair dead still. His face looked at the ceiling above the gaping wound.

Two whores screamed. Everyone at our table pushed back all at once. "Geezuz!" Barber yelled, turning away from the table. Wilbur reached for his unloaded pistol. Barber and the gent on the other side of Letsky dove for the floor—quick crawling in opposite directions. I leaped up banging my knee. The table wobbled precariously. Paprete said, *"Hah,"* and pushed Letsky forward. His head hit the table and bounced. Wild Bill's final ghastly noise sounded like a suffering busted-up horse being put down. His face and cheek lay in a growing pool of blood.

Paprete roared his presence in the saloon like an enraged grizzly, holding his knife high, triumphant. I feared the breed would scalp Letsky's corpse. Thankfully, a table lay between us. Paprete dared anyone to reach for the money he felt he had earned. His smell drifted over me again. He licked the knife and spat blood on the floor. His eyes were glassy, and he wiped a crimson streak on his sleeve. Paprete sensed someone and whirled quickly, the knife extended menacingly. Dubois swung his club, shattering Paprete's knife hand. A second blow on the breed's skull broke the axe handle. Paprete crumpled, sliding down the back of Letsky's chair as if gut shot. Still eyeing the skinner's bloody head, Dubois kicked at the knife. It skittered through the sawdust covered floor like a nimble lizard, bouncing sideways off a spittoon.

The once lively Gold Shoe began to empty as other tables cashed out, and Letsky bled out in front of me. Gawkers came over to our table to peek at Letsky's corpse on their way out.

It seemed like a long time, but within moments, Sheriff Billy Ray Keeley came in and Dubois pointed to us. He and Dubois grabbed Paprete by the armpits and dragged him through the sawdust used to soak up booze and tobacco spit and out the door. Paprete's head left a smeared blood trail through the sawdust.

I picked up the part of the pot not dripping Letsky's blood–didn't need another bloody face haunting me and didn't care who came for Letsky's body. I didn't want any part of it.

Leaning against the back wall of the saloon staring at Letsky a mite longer than I ought to time moved like molasses.Sliding past the bar and out the back door into the alley, I doubled over, my insides emptying onto a stack of empty wooden whiskey crates. The liquor vomit burned like a branding iron. I gazed up at the expanse of the night sky hoping for relief among the stars.

You ain't gonna like them cards.

What possessed Letsky to say that? His pride? Something else?

I lingered out behind the Shoe for a half hour leaning against an empty barrel. My eyes fixated on the moon chasing the morning star in a ceaseless planetary dance.

The longer I stayed, phantoms began emerging from within the moon. Each new face marred by battle scars from a bitter conflict long ago. The faces were familiar. My men's blue uniforms were stained blood red. They stared at me from within an icy black depth, lifeless as stones, not moving, there being no breath left in them. They were dead. Like Letsky.

LETSKY DIDN'T GET much of a sendoff. Most folks in Grant's Crossing didn't know him. They asked me to say a few words since I was the last lawyer seen talking to him. I declined. A funeral pastor ought to do the word-saying. But no one ever saw Letsky in any of the town's churches, so they handed him over to the Masons to offer up a bit of their peculiar dignity before burying him.

The Masons had a peculiar rule book about the unchurched. A funeral required dignity, and the Masons provided it so long as a group, like the Sequoyah County bar, ponied up a collection for two Masons to dig a proper grave. A wordy eulogy came from Dr. J. T. M. Howell. Letsky, he said, had pursued "knowledge and truth before all else." I tried to remember when Howell might have known Letsky or Letsky might have mentioned this theological pursuit in order for Howell to make such a bald-faced claim. I'd never met a deep-thinking Letsky. But as the only member of the county bar at Letsky's funeral pretending to listen, I began wondering what I'd missed.

When Howell finally took his seat, the Knights of Pythias and the Pythian Sisters, chief mourners in a ceremony resembling a church but no one understood, shook their tambourines like they were sending a raucous soul to the dark edge of the world or places better left unspoken.

A day or so after the murder the city hired a stonecutter to prepare his gravestone with his name and the words, *"Murdered April 13th, 1888."* The stone man said life had swamped him and it'd be a while before a stone could be laid on the grave. Meanwhile, Paprete rotted in jail waiting for Sequoyah County to appoint him a lawyer before going through the motions of a trial. Taking Paprete's case wouldn't earn a lawyer any praise or make him the town's top gavel jack. And even if a lawyer managed the impossible and got Paprete off, the breed couldn't save himself from the anger out there. Bets were taken at the opera house window on exactly how long it would take before the vigilantes got to Paprete.

Three weeks after they dragged Paprete from the Golden Shoe and tossed him into a jail cell, the town's patience wore thin. A rough as a cob mob decided they'd save the county the expense of a trial. They shoved aside the two deputies who barely put up a fight and hauled Paprete out. His protests drowned in their resolve. No one bothered asking why he killed Letsky. It didn't matter. Three strong men pinned Paprete down, binding his hands tight. A fourth slipped a noose around his neck. Without a word, they hoisted him high on a telegraph pole. His legs kicked out in desperation, but the rope did its work silencing him for good. Paprete's end came as harsh as the life he'd lived and the death he'd dealt to Letsky. A half-breed had killed a white man. In their eyes, justice had been served. The crowd, staring up at Paprete's swaying body, had nothing more to say.

The men who lynched Paprete were treated to drinks at the Golden Shoe, and two Masons were paid to dump his body in the ground. Without other instructions, they buried Paprete close to where Letsky lay. There were no markers or a stone. The topsoil left its body lost to the earth without a trace of who lay beneath it.

Judge Powell asked me to go through Letsky's things and see if any cash lay stashed in a local bank or his things. If so, I would look for kinfolk who ought to claim it. If any were found, I could open a probate and take a modest fee. I sifted through what little Letsky had and found nothing of value. No money and no family. The remnants of his life were few.

When the stonecutter finally finished Letsky's marker, he hitched it to a dead wagon behind two mules and hauled it out to the cemetery. A yard man told me later the cutter stood there squinting at the two unmarked graves, maybe trying to recall which one held Letsky. After a quick glance, he stared at the yard man and set the stone in place on the grave he figured was the right one. He made a guess. However, nobody would dig up the body to be certain.

A year went by and those two graves lay side by side. One with Letsky's name etched in stone. The other as blank as the grass and weeds growing on the mound. The Kansas prairie didn't care for markers or names. It took both men's bodies and dismembered them into the soil. Memories were left in the wind.

—Dean Halliday Smith is the pen name of Ron Smith, a fifth-generation Kansan, a native of Manhattan, a retired attorney after 46 years was a former

general counsel of the Kansas Bar Association, and who served on a governor's staff. His farm is near the excellent preserved NPS site at Fort Larned. He is a Vietnam veteran and a civil war historian and a grandfather. He has written a variety of historical articles about 19th century lawyers for the Journal of the Kansas Bar Association *and a published biography of Thomas Ewing Jr., the state's first chief justice, published by the University of Missouri Press as part of their prestigious Blue and Grey series. Smith's Civil War novel,* The Wastage *was released in 2018. A second novel,* A Twisted Path to Justice, *about a historic murder trial set in 1888 Kansas, is in his agent's hands making the rounds of New York publishers.*

Smith is a regular contributor to the opinions page of the Kansas Reflector *and newspapers across the state. One of the articles in late 2023 was the most downloaded article of the year.*

The Scout by Charles Marion Russell

TENNER

BLANCHE DESCHAIN

"LANDS SAKES!" ISABELLE swallowed down a hiss of pain. She lifted her finger closer, squinted at the bit of glass, and forced her eyes to narrow. Her eyesight had gone a bit blurry this last year. The details and edges of things had softened. The shard finally worked free, and a bead of blood welled up beneath it. She struggled to hold in a sigh as her eyes finished their task and fell on her son.

Arcadia's blue eyes were wide and round as he watched her. He sat hunched in on himself—hands fisted-tight in his lap. His dog, Tenner, cowered beneath the chair. A furry white lump quivered in the shadows. The pair had dashed a mad retreat to the corner after they shattered her prized Lacy Glass dish. Around them, shards of cobalt-blue littered the ground strewn with the last of the autumn season's pecans.

She knew the boy feared she would let her temper best her as she'd done in the past. His heavy regard was enough to drive her mad. She couldn't stay here, feeling judged any longer. She rose, padded to the door, and pulled her thick wool coat from the peg. Arcadia's face lit up when he realized she had a smile for him. He snatched his hat from her hand and tugged it on.

"Let's see how the traps are, boy. We could use some air."

She pulled open the cedar-plank door to spill boy, dog and herself into the watery, late winter light. The sun was hidden behind a haze that paled the sky to a milky shade of blue-white. She smiled to herself as Arcadia and Tenner ran ahead.

Her boy had showed up with that dog near on two years ago. The little thing had been dirty-brown, raw-boned, and starving on his sled. She'd been halfway to sure the animal was already dead. At Arcadia's urging, she'd accepted the shallow rise and fall of its chest as proof of life. In the end, she'd agreed to nurse the poor creature to health.

On a sunny day, the first of summer's heat, they bathed the dog with rose-scented washing soap, and the boy named him. She had been amazed, and a little proud, to see the dog's skinny form fill out and his beautiful white coat shine in the sunlight. Tenner was most often found splayed before the cabin's crackling fire, but he was a good hunter, too. She'd never had a rat from the first day he'd been well enough to walk.

Her boy was coltish now, almost thirteen. The pair of them looked as if they could run for days and never tire. She grimaced as Tenner slipped in a slick of mud and took the pair down in a mud-locked tussle. Isabelle tried to hide her smile as she watched their antics, but the expression faded into a frown as she found the last trap missing.

The other traps had been empty. One had been disturbed by some creature. Bits of fur and scarlet drops of blood were left around the twisted snare. Her larder would struggle to supply this winter if her traps didn't start providing. She'd enjoyed the walk. They laughed and chatted the way they used to. She slung an arm fondly around the boy's shoulder—tried to appreciate this moment, as she often forgot to do.

Some time later, a dawning awareness took her when she gauged their distance from the homestead. She looked to the sky with concern. It was almost dusk now. Gray-bellied clouds rolled in from the east heavy with snow. With a sickening jolt, she felt the lack of her rifle. She'd left it at the cabin in her haste. She cursed herself for a distracted old fool. With crooked fingers to her lips, she whistled loudly and started back home. The crackling undergrowth spit forth boy and dog in a loud pile of wool, fur, and sharp holly leaves.

"How does hot milk sound before bed?"

He opened his mouth to reply, and she saw an unknown expression cross his face. She followed his gaze and saw a muscled hulk stir in the shadows only a few feet away. Her failing vision had betrayed her, and the cloak of dusk-shadow had done her in. A specter of death and hell, a huge bear, rose from a deep patch of shadow in a bramble thicket to their left.

A deep rumbling bellow ripped from the creature. The sound was primeval and visceral. The echoes of its roar blasted the strength itself from her soul, shook her teeth in their gums, and filled the woods with the scent of terror. Leaves rained down as frightened birds burst from the darkened forest and shrieked away into the safety of the violet sky above them.

For a moment, she stood frozen. She knew the creature would turn now and tear the guts from her body with a clawed swipe. A scream filled the air around her. She did not approve of hysterics and was chagrined to realize the brittle sound had torn its way from her own throat. A spike of fear had tacked her lungs shut. The lack of air blackened her vision before it slammed her wits back into her body.

Isabelle tore her eyes from the bear and pushed the boy behind her. She turned back to face the creature. At eight feet, it loomed above her. Its round ears brushing the dome of the sky, loomed higher than the branches of the small pine trees. A blur of white pummeled into the bear from behind, and she gasped, falling back against Arcadia. It was Tenner.

The dog moved quick as lightning, darted away, and tore by again with sharp nips that turned the bear's lumbering head away. Tenner dodged a swipe of the massive paw with a whine. The whites of his eyes shone as he looked to Isabelle for aid she couldn't give.

He didn't flag as he sprinted past again, farther away now. He was leading the bear away. Tenner drew up behind the bear and wrapped his paws around its stout torso. He dug his teeth in the thick, shaggy fur. The bear stumbled back—claws razored down. The pair vanished from view locked in their embrace. They slid down a shallow gully in a tumble of leaves and icy mud. Snarls split the blackness of the night.

Isabelle fell back as Arcadia tried to rush past her to the little white dog's side. With a hand fisted deep in the gray wool of his jacket, she heaved with all her strength and pulled her boy back through the trees. She had to fight him once as the growls of the dog and the enraged snarls of the bear sounded through the woods. He couldn't understand the value of the gift Tenner had given her, but she wouldn't squander it. She hardened her heart and picked the boy up and threw him over her shoulder. Roughly she heaved him up the steps and into the warmth of the cabin.

"If you want to see me or that dog alive again, you stay put. Do you hear me, boy?"

She didn't wait for his reply. She had raised him right. With heavy hands, numb from the tussle and the ice-edged snow, she grabbed the rifle from above the door. She left no time for thought as she threw herself down the steps into the darkness and snow far beyond the warm light of home. Branches slapped at her face, and cold snow slid down the back of her jacket as she made her way toward the snarls.

She cursed every second the snow tugged at her boots, every branch that snagged and wouldn't let her aid such a loyal friend. The growls went silent, and the echoing nothing of the forest filled her with despair. Ahead, to her right, she heard a splintering crash. A monstrous form pushed its way through the tree shadow. She froze and waited a long while until the forest was quiet again.

Finally, she pushed her way into the clearing where she had seen Tenner make his last stand. Great swaths of raw white wood and splintered broken branches marred the wrecked trees. The air stunk of animal musk and sharp pine sap. She didn't see Tenner.

For the next two hours, she followed the path of the bear's destructive run where it met the edge of the river. As she stepped into a patch of moonlight, light shimmered down through the trees and illuminated a curled lump of white against the fallen leaves and torn snow.

She ran and knelt down beside Tenner, praying that he would still be alive. Her heart was in her throat as she ran a hand through the red-slicked fur. Tears ran down her cheeks when a steady thumping sounded through the forest muted against the snow. It was Tenner's wagging tail.

She held in a gasp as she looked over the extent of the dog's injuries. Tenner's flanks and sides were rubbed raw. One of his legs was a pulp of white fur and red. The injuries hurt to look upon. Ever loyal, he tried to clean the blood from her hands with gentle licks as she felt his skull for injuries.

Carefully, she slid Tenner onto the sled she'd brought along and dragged him back to the house. The rough hemp rope dug deep into her shoulders. The boy was waiting in the doorway. His eyesight better than hers by a league. She decided she would teach him to nurse Tenner and do other work around the cabin. It was time he learned. Hell, she was forgetting her gun in the woods at dark. It was well past time.

Isabelle looked back to the sled and the dog's limp form. She smiled, despite the tears that left icy tracks down her cheeks. They would come through this all right, her, the boy, and the dog. Between the three of them they could take care of themselves.

—————————

—Blanche Deschain writes books about the women that live inside her barbarous mind. Strong, strapping women, fox-clever females, hero-women that step in, when the world has become too wild. Her passion for the west was ignited when she moved to Utah to live with her grandmother, an avid genealogist. This wise-woman imparted a love and a passion for giving life to the stories we tell ourselves.

Blanche has a short story accepted for publication in a winter anthology Greed, Gold and Gunsmoke. *She also writes poetry about the spirituality, religion and darkness that inhabits the red earth of the deep South. She has a book of poetry titled* Bury Me In the Red Clay.

Before she started writing short stories and poetry, Blanche got a Bachelors in Zoology and Plant Biology from NC State University. After that, just to see how the cat jumped, she worked as a 911 dispatcher and a wildlife rescuer. She is a jewelry maker, baker, herbalist, quilter, and witch in her spare time.

Blanche currently resides on beautiful Vancouver Island with her husband and daughter.

California or Oregan by Frank Tenney Johnson

REGARDING THE REGRETTABLE PASSING OF J.J. O'ROURKE

T.I. MITCHELL

WHEN THE ROOF of his beloved mine all but fell on top of him, James John O'Rourke dared not believe it. It was already August in Nevada. Late summer. He was digging his claim. He was ever and always digging. It was before supper but not yet time to quit. He was digging when the mountain made a quiet rumble that became a sound as unholy as a cannonade. Crackling as it went, it snapped and thundered, tumbling and jolting. Finally, the noise dissipated, and the shaking ebbed away. Moist air and dust settled around him as he crouched with his hands over his head. There were rocks on the floor next to him. He turned from the face of the mine to examine the gravity of the collapse behind him. At least his lantern had not failed. He could see more rocks and soil had come down close, bursting into the stulm and so filling it. The space was now packed with all kinds of detritus. By close inspection and gentle probing, he knew a good deal of the cavity beyond the entrance, up to thirty feet of it, had caved in and he was trapped beyond it far inside.

He shook his head, not ready to believe he was sealed within the earth, betrayed by his own handiwork. His mine. He had always been so considerate with her. He had measured her length gently, digging her walls with the consistency and care of a lover. He had firmly braced her walls with every progress and had not overused his blasting powder. He had always said his prayers for her each night, making orderly plans together on the side of the mountain with the clarity of sunrise. Yet, he was here in the quarter light caught within her cool embrace. By his estimation, there was only ten feet of clean mine shaft remaining. A clear space four foot across and six foot high with little but fetid air trapped inside. He himself was uninjured but already sore and stiff from countless days working underground. What could he do now? Dig his way backwards into the unstable mountainside to get out? He stared at the ceiling above him. Would this also hold? The thought made him angry. This mine had the best of him. He had bled for her, paying in hard cash for the claim, honest money he had earned while fighting alongside General Sheridan in '63. He had furnished her with materials and luxuries he had purchased by taking out loans from the clean-suited men who flourished in the cities. Then he had put in labor, months of labor. And for what? Was she so ungrateful? He had denied himself for her with little comfort beyond the hope he would discover the glorious riches she held buried in her depths. He had even named her for Our Lady of Lourdes, and he hoped she would bless his endeavours. But if that foreign saint heard him now, there was no answer. The air inside the passage was past quiet. No one would find him and there were no friends waiting outside to hear him if he cried for rescue.

It had been his choice to work alone. He knew that. He did not want to share his spoils. The seam he hoped to find had promised riches that would cover not only his debts but also give him new opportunities far away from this life. All his wishes and hopes for reward were now as good as gone. There would be no one and nobody to miss him on the side of this nameless mountain. It was only a day's ride from Virginia City, but may as well be on the edge of the universe. Not even the Mormon missionaries would seek him here. His knees bent, and he sagged to the floor. God willing, he could think up some way to get out. He had his pickaxe and shovel, but he did not have his blasting powder or fuses. They were laying idle down the slope at his encampment. There was enough oil for his lamp to last several days but he didn't have much water and only some tack and dried meat he had brought wrapped in his jacket.

Perhaps this was all God's way to test his faith? He had survived the war with the Confederates hadn't he? They had not killed him for all their intent. Surely, he had only to use the gifts God had given him to get out of jeopardy again. He leaned back and rested against the wall, breathing deep and trying to imagine what recourse he might have. While he busied his mind, he closed his eyes to block out the blackness surrounding him. There was no hope that could be easily found in this dark corner. With his hands clenched tight in his lap and the growing stiffness in his jaw, he knew his thoughts were merely stifling the panic he could feel rising in his chest. If only he had his pipe, he could think clearer.

"God, please let me find a way to get out from this place," he said into the silence. There was no response. He opened his eyes and stared up at the ceiling, willing himself not to shout. Was God listening?

"Lord, I promise to give a half of what I find to your church."

The silence engulfed him. He stood up and started to claw at the debris. Fingers scraped against rocks, catching on edges hidden in the dark. He cursed this unseen foe and fetched his shovel, starting to dig out larger quantities, his breathing fast and desperate. But as he cleared a little earth, more fell in. A section of timbers in the remaining space now began to sag. He stood back, tears running hot down the dirt on his face and neck. The light from his lantern was his only comfort. Had even God forgotten him? He moved deeper into the shaft—sweat running down his back and arms. He dropped his tools together, their clatter in the narrow space, dull and without echo. He picked up some remaining timber to strengthen the braces he had dislodged and continued working until he had secured the little space he had left. His mine. Faithless mistress. She still needed him.

When he had used up all the remaining timber, he sat down heavily once more. Resolute but faint, the lantern's illumination could barely reach the edges of the chamber.

"Please, dear God...." He didn't know what else to ask so the sentence remained unfinished, no more than a dry hole. He took the food from his jacket, his battered hands shaking as he did so. The morsels were dry and flavourless. He washed them down with some of the water and wished again for his pipe and the brandy he kept at the bottom of his haversack. If he was going to die, he wanted to have at least one last, fitting, final supper. Didn't even the condemned have this? Instead, he finished what remained of the food, said his nightly prayers because it was his custom, and curled up on the rocky floor. Even buried under a mountain, sleep found him.

When he woke, there was pain in every extremity. His limbs wailed and his head ached. Every inch of his body was stiff. He had found meager rest on the hard and uneven surface but without a timepiece or the sun to tell him the time he didn't know for how long. There was no give inside the mountain. Yet in all his agonies, he felt a weight had been lifted. Was it brain fever? Or the lack of clean air? He couldn't fathom it. All he knew with certainty was that he didn't want to die alone in this hole, and that thought... that singular thought... had given him back his hope. He wanted to breathe the fresh mountain air again and see the light of the sun. He wanted to know day from night and to taste proper food. With God or without, he would do it.

The next sound that James John O'Rourke heard was a dog barking. The sound was above him in an unseen outside world. He shouted at it and the barking stopped. The air was too thin. He thought perhaps he had imagined it. Then it started again. It truly was a dog. A brute with a large bark, and it was directly above him. He wasn't mistaken, but he was confused. He didn't have a dog. How was it there? All he had was a mule. That was tied up safely, he hoped, at the encampment along with all his gear, his rifle and ammunition, his winter coat and boots, the tent and his blankets, and all the food he now sorely missed.

The dog had stopped barking again. Did it belong to one of the Washoe people? He called out.

"Help." There was no response. He picked up his shovel and thrust the handle into the ceiling, banging it against the rock. "Help, help me, please."

His voice was broken. A dry rasp. There was no response, but a little of the ceiling fell down onto his face. Dirt and damp soil ran over his forehead, kissing his cheeks and nose, and bumping against his lips. Small rocks harmlessly fellnext to his feet like sand through a glass timer. Then, he heard the dog again. It was not so close now, but his attention was distracted from it. He felt something else. A breeze? The air was certainly less stale where he stood. He thrust the shovel handle up again and stepped back as larger rocks dislodged and landed next to him, brushing roughly past his arms and shoulders. They smashed into the lantern extinguishing the flame. The darkness was now complete, yet hope was growing. He could feel the air moving. He turned the shovel around and pushed it up into the ceiling. More soil and rocks came down. They struck him. These were unkind and bruising. He kept his eyes closed against them, turning his face down to one side. He could die this way. Crushed by the very metals he sought. His instinct was to be more careful, to take things more slowly, but he knew it was carefulness that had brought him here. He pushed up, reckless now, abandoned in his efforts. He pushed up, up towards heaven, swatting at God and Our Lady of Lourdes with his shovel, struggling with his grip on the handle, struggling also with shallow breathing and his strength fading.

At last, there was nothing to strike against. He swung at air. It was empty and fresh. He dropped the shovel and dared to open his eyes. Where there was air, there was also light. It peeked through the shadows of the large trees above. Shafts of life-giving light were just above him, no more than six feet from where he was half-buried in the mountainside. He saw the light had color as he crawled up towards it and out of the earth. It was white and green and blue and warm and had a store of life held within it. It came down to where he was and dazzled his eyes, softening his face, and stroking his hands as he crawled further up the slope into it, further out of the mine and to the edge of the hole. Resting now, he soaked in it. The light was joyful, playing in trees that were burnished green. Some of the leaves had already started to bronze. He could hear the wind in the branches, jangling and clanking. There were other noises too. Silver-tongued birds and rusty crickets sang out. They didn't know the fear of the underground, just freedom and the outside world. He felt the stones at the edge of the pit underneath him. Even they were rounded and warmed by the sun. And beyond everything, high up above, gilded clouds floated past serenely, their shining faces unaware of his mute wonder.

"It's regrettable, but he's gone. We can't bring him back from the dead."

The voice broke his reverie. He didn't recognise the owner. It was close—perhaps only a stone's throw away.

"He still owes me." He recognized this one. It was Richardson, one of the men from Virginia City who had loaned him plenty of money. He remembered he had promised to pay Richardson long before June was over.

"If you want to stay here and dig him out, it's your right." The unfamiliar voice spoke again.

He pulled himself up out of the remains of the destroyed mine and lay among the boulders that had come down the mountain. He peered around the edge of them, looking down to where the voices floated up.

There were three men. They were there by the entrance of his mine, standing back aways from the disordered land all around, frowning at the enormity of the landslide that had come down from further up the valley. One of them was Richardson. The other two he didn't know. Each was armed with pistols, and one carried a rifle. The tallest one wore the hat of a Confederate officer and smoked a short cigar. He spoke next.

"You can see there's no way in or out, Mister. God took this Yankee before we could."

"But he owes money. And interest on the dollar." Richardson stared at the mouth of the mine. Her lips sealed shut—secrets kept. If he only looked upwards, he might see who he had come for. But his eyes stayed on the mine, his own mind deep with his financial concerns. The other two turned around.

"Let's take what we can from his belongings and go," the man in the soldier's hat said. "Then you can pay us what you owe for this day's misadventure. We still have enough daylight to make it back to town."

"But my money...." Richardson said, turning to follow.

Further down the hill, beyond the devastation, there were four horses waiting. They were tied up next to his mule. A large brown dog sniffed around the campfire.

He watched them go down into his camp. He thought about crying out for their help but was not sure that they would bring it to him. So, he stayed quiet and waited. He watched as the two strangers went through his things, sharing his brandy between them as they went, laughing as they lifted up his precious Sharps, a prize he had kept from Shenandoah. Richardson declined their offers of the brandy and put a saddle on the mule, loading it up with boxes of the remaining black powder, wire, and fuses. He went back and forth busily from the tent while the others drank and smoked, taking out the blankets and the remaining canned goods too. He put these into a sack and tied it all to the mule's back. The dog looked bored and wandered back towards the mine, sniffing the air and looking up the valley toward him. Just as he thought it would discover him, the man in the Confederate hat called out, and the dog turned back. It trotted down to the camp, tail wagging freely. When it reached its master, the man gave it a strip of dried meat from a sack that was tied up high on a tree. Even though he felt desperate with hunger, he didn't begrudge the animal for its reward. It must be the dog he had heard.

Then, he waited in silence and watched them all ride out. Three men, four horses, his mule, and the dog following behind. They had come for him and gone away with only the remaining traces of his life. Up here in the ruins of his mine, he was still safe from their reach. He stretched out his limbs in the sun. In an hour or so, when he was sure they were not coming back, he would go down, gather what was left of his belongings and head east. He would need to give up his name and find a new way to earn a living, but that could wait. For now, he had the light, and it was enough.

—T.I. Mitchell lives in Auckland, New Zealand where he works as a technical writer for a company making commercial refrigeration technology. His crime novel, Good Cop, Bad Cop, *(Rogue Monster Press, 2016) was co-written with his friend Angus Gillies under the pen name Angus Mitchell. His short fiction and poetry have appeared in a number of journals including* 100 New Zealand Short Short Stories, Plots with Guns, Pulp Magazine, The Outpost, *and several of Akashic Publishing's online series. This is his first story with a western setting.*

WORDS OF WARNING

THOMAS WHITE

AVAILA LOOMER WAS sitting with a book in her lap, but she was no longer reading. Jasmine Trent, the Quaker widow Availa was visiting, and Jasmine's son, Crayfield, were standing by the kitchen table. All three were wide-eyed.

Standing just inside the Trent cabin was Kent Bascomb. He was tall and wide with raised, pale scars on his neck and the left side of his face. Behind him, stood two men with grim expressions. They were as dirty as the man they rode in with.

After he looked around the well-built home, Bascomb returned to the women. Jasmine shuddered once again. Her hand on Cray's shoulder was not protection, but it was another way for his mother to assure herself he was safe for now.

"Real nice place," Bascomb said. "But sort of far from Creek Bend."

Jasmine drew Cray closer to her.

Bascomb saw the worried mother's move, but Availa had his attention. "Are you living out here, Miss Loomer?"

Availa shook her head. "No."

"Visiting an old friend?"

A nod was her only reply.

"I see you're still one for the books. Is Stella Trace still at the school?"

Availa nodded again, but she was no longer wide-eyed. "For now she is."

Her reply was stronger than the last because of the hatred she had for the man that threatened them.

"You'll be taking over?"

"I'll be the new teacher, Bascomb."

They glared at one another for a long moment, and then Bascomb returned to Jasmine.

"Does your visitor help with Crayfield?" he venomously asked.

"She has but not today," Jasmine stammered.

Bascomb considered the youth. "He looks like his father. And if he has the same mind that help should be every day. When a man drinks and blabs after he cashes in the gold dust he finds, he's asking for the trouble that always answers."

Jasmine's jaw trembled as her eyes grew red. Cray sullenly looked at the floor.

"What do you want, Bascomb?" Availa asked, now on the edge of her chair.

Bascomb turned to her with his eyes narrowed. The pause was almost unbearable for the Trents.

"I want Marshal Slater face down out there, Miss Loomer. And now with your help...."

Availa looked at Jasmine and Cray and then returned to Bascomb. The two men behind him looked at one another but neither spoke.

"You won't ask me why you'd help me. You just looked at the reason."

Availa only glared at him.

Bascomb nodded at the man to his left. "I was going to send Deviax into town to tell Slater that if he wanted to see the Trents alive again, he was to ride out here alone. Now, he'll be told that you're out here... hurt."

As Jasmine put her arm around Cray's neck and pressed him to her, she looked at Availa, who was still defiant.

"I'm not surprised," Availa said with no stammer. "Caleb ran you out of Creek Bend three years ago. He was a brand new marshal, but you... all of you... couldn't stand up to him and his deputies. That's where your scars are from."

Bascomb bristled and took a step forward as if about to lunge at her. "Maybe it shouldn't be just a story, Miss Loomer."

"Maybe your story will end as badly now as it did then, Bascomb."

"Please, Availa," Jasmine said, stepping back to the kitchen counter. Cray, still in tow, went with her.

Jasmine's worried expression only strengthened her plea, but Availa's expression was set in the same mask of defiance. And Availa was looking only at Bascomb who was now standing halfway between her and the front door.

Deviax and the other man, Benson, looked at one another again. They were still grim but amused by the woman's courage.

"You'll be his downfall, Miss Loomer," Bascomb spat. "His story ends with you."

Availa smiled as if a sharp reply would be easy and immediate. But the moment she looked once again at Jasmine and Cray, the fiery young woman only slid back in the chair to sit as she had while reading.

Bascomb gave his order. "Deviax, ride into town to the hotel. You'll see an old prospector with suspenders and a hat too big for his head. He'll be spitting from his chaw wherever it pleases him—Red Yates by name. He's always around there this time of day. Tell him Availa Loomer is out here hurt."

Long moments passed and then Bascomb nodded to himself as if pleased with a decision.

"There was an accident. Miss Loomer's buckboard horse was spooked by a snake and ran. She fell into that rock pile out front. She's got an arm she can't move, and she's bleeding from the head. Falls asleep and wakes and talks to herself."

Bascomb looked at Deviax who nodded that he understood. Benson seemed relieved that it was not his memory in question. He had already scratched his forehead and shrugged.

Their confident leader returned to Availa. "Throw me the book, Miss Loomer. Deviax will take it with him."

"I will?" Deviax rasped. He sounded like his throat was as dry as the dirt they wore from riding in.

Bascomb spun on his heels. "Yes, you will."

Benson eased away from Deviax.

"You're going to tell Yates that she wants Slater to have the book because she may not see him again. He's one for books, too. And for her. It's another way to tell him how bad she is."

Deviax's nod of agreement was hardly evident, but it sufficed.

Bascomb turned back to Availa, and she threw the book with only enough strength for it to land in his calloused hands.

Deviax took the book from Bascomb and slid it into the inside pocket of his jacket.

"Ride back right after you talk to Yates," Bascomb said. "Then I'll tell the two of you where to wait for Slater and Doc Dawson. Somebody's hurt, so he'll ride out with the marshal.

I'll wait here with the ladies and the young man."

Jasmine's jaw trembled once again. She had such a tight hold on Cray that he grabbed her hand in protest. Availa only sat and glared.

Bascomb sneered. "We'll be listening for the gunshots."

<hr />

MARSHAL CALEB SLATER sat down in his desk chair, but before he continued his paperwork, he allowed himself some personal thoughts.

Nice enough girl that Lyna Blayland. She's not leaving Creek Bend now that her father's the new owner of the saloon. And she'd take up with a lawman. Told me as much.

But she's not Availa Loomer, who won't take up with a lawman. And she told me as much. Plain enough too.

Slater shook his head as if it would rid him of all thoughts except for the ones about his stack of papers.

So, with his pen in one hand and the top sheet from the stack in the other, he was underway with another part of his job he never shunned. He was always organized and precise.

The office door flew open and Red Yates stumbled in letting the momentum of the backswing nearly close the door. He had a book in one hand.

"Marshal," he said, almost gasping. He skidded to a stop in front of the desk. "Miss Loomer's bad hurt. She's out at the Trent place. Fell on the rocks. Man rode out and told me. He was riding by the place when Missus Trent called to him. She didn't want to leave Crayfield alone with Miss Loomer."

Slater left the paperwork and rolled back in his chair. "Slow down, Red."

"But from what that man said, Marshal, she's real bad, and..."

Slater stood up, tall and slim. "Red."

Yates was silent under the Marshal's gaze.

"Keep it simple and slow, Red. You're not surrounded in the saloon."

The deflating Yates nodded.

But Slater continued. "I know you can tell me the right way, Red, and I heard what you already said. Who was the man?"

The old prospector nodded his thanks and then paused before he tried again.

"Never seen him, Marshal. But he said Miss Loomer's real bad. Falls asleep then wakes. It's hard to understand some of what she says. Missus Trent doesn't know if Doc Dawson can help, but he's to ride out, too. Miss Loomer wants to see you. But if you're not in time, she wants you to have this."

He handed the book to Slater.

Slater took it, turned it over, and then opened the front cover to slowly page through it. Yates waited.

After stopping for some long moments at one of the pages, Slater looked up but did not speak.

"What is it, Marshal?"

He answered with some reluctance. "It's my journal."

Yates's expression was his question, but he asked it regardless. "You keep a journal?"

"I used to. When I first took this job. But I haven't for some time."

"What's she doing with your journal?"

Yates stepped back to reprimand himself for a question he knew he should not have asked.

Slater did not answer the question. But only a moment later, he spoke with the authority for which he was well known.

"They're all in trouble, Red. Go tell Jack Henry and Trap Abner I want them here now. I'll tell Doc Dawson. He's next door."

"All right, Marshal. But how do you know they're all in trouble? Did Miss Loomer write something in your journal?"

"She didn't add a word. Just trust me."

Yates ran out as fast as he ran in.

BASCOMB WAS SITTING at the end of the kitchen table closest to the front door. Now supremely confident because of the gunshots they heard not long ago, he alternated his gaze from Availa, still in the same chair, to Jasmine and Cray, who were now standing by the side window and close to their unwelcome visitor. Cray was nearly behind his mother.

"Creek Bend needs a new marshal and doctor," Bascomb said, his mouth stained muddy. "So, what do I do with you three?" He spat once again on the floor.

Availa stayed as she was, but Jasmine took a step back and Cray went with her.

Bascomb let them worry for long moments from the answers their fear gave them.

"I'm going to leave you here," he said at last, rid of his own worries. "Tell your story. It won't matter. We'll disappear into the hills before Henry and Abner can ride out. Unless they rode out with the marshal and Creek Bend needs new deputies, too."

He leaned forward and sneered at Availa. "I hope your book wasn't shot up, Miss Loomer. Would that be worse than losing Slater?"

Availa sprang to her feet, her eyes flaring. But before she could speak, she heard a hoarse, threatening voice.

"Bascomb."

The one named stood and looked out the side window. The other three looked as well.

"Bascomb," the voice said again, just as hoarse and threatening.

A man staggered in front of the window and fell forward landing in the dirt.

"That's Dawson," Bascomb said, more to himself than his captives. He stepped toward the window. "How did he walk away from...?"

The question ended when a boot threw open the front door and in ran a lawman with a rifle dead set on Bascomb.

"Don't try it, Bascomb," Slater commanded. "Just let the gun belt fall behind you and walk out with your hands way up. And keep that mouth shut."

Slater stepped close enough to the kitchen table for Bascomb to do only what he was told. His sneer reduced to a decoration for defeat.

Outside, Henry bound the captive's hands while Abner guaranteed he would not disappear into the hills.

Inside, Slater spoke to their help. "It's all right, Doc. And thanks."

Doc Dawson stood up and brushed off his jacket before he looked in the window.

"Perhaps I should retire for the theater," he said, his voice clear and welcoming.

SLATER AND AVAILA were standing outside the Trent home. In the distance, Henry and Abner were leading Bascomb back to Creek Bend. Henry rode in front of the captive's horse and Abner behind. And behind Abner, were the deceased Benson and Deviax, each stomach down across his horse's saddle.

Availa looked once again at Jasmine and Cray who were still cleaning everything stained by Bascomb. When Availa turned back to Slater, he spoke first.

"Where did you find my journal?"

"Near the saloon after you and Clem Halstrom... had it out."

Slater nodded. "That was some night. I'm scarred because of it."

He raised his left hand. A jagged scar ran across the first three knuckles.

Availa only blinked a look at the hand. "The journal was falling apart and some of the pages were smudged. I was going to return it the next day, but then I had to stand in for three weeks at the school in Dry Stream. At night, I rewrote it in a new journal, and I've been rereading the new one. Yours is in my bag. I would have returned it last night, but then I stopped here."

"I recognized your handwriting."

Availa nodded. "I thought you would. I also thought you would look through the early pages wondering why your words were in my journal. So while Bascomb was talking to Deviax about taking the book with him, I circled the word Bascomb the first time you wrote it to turn it into a black eye. Only Jasmine and Cray saw me."

Slater nearly smiled. "That was my warning of the trouble. Good thing I wrote about running him out of town. I left my journal in the pocket of an old jacket I didn't think I'd wear again. But then, the one I was wearing was soaked when I rode back to town in that rain storm. I was wearing the old one when Halstrom shot up the saloon, and then I couldn't find the journal afterwards."

"Good thing about Bascomb and Halstrom," Availa said. And then, startled, she adjusted. "I mean about Halstrom that you ran him out too."

"I know what you meant, Availa. And it's a good thing Bascomb isn't as smart as he thinks he is. I suspected an ambush. And we know this territory better than his likes ever will. Henry and Abner found his men, and there was some trouble. But Henry and Abner are good. They're real good. And then I found Bascomb. Now, there's no more trouble."

Slater admired her before he continued. "Thank you."

Availa smiled. "I'll give you your journal back when we're back in Creek Bend."

"I'd be obliged."

"And maybe we should talk about what we talked about before."

Surprised, Slater considered her. "You said you wouldn't take up with a lawman."

Availa lowered her eyes. "There was some trouble. But then, I read a lawman's journal."

She looked up and admired him. "Now, there's no more trouble."

———————

—Thomas White wrote this short story as his first Western submitted to a publication. For many years he has written amateur pulp fiction short stories just for the sake of writing them. His reading includes short stories by Louis L'Amour and Zane Grey.

He received a Ph.D. in the social sciences. A former general education college professor, he taught undergraduate survey courses and included introductory film studies in many of his courses with emphasis on classic feature films spanning the silent era to the early 1960s. Westerns and noir films were prominent. With no claim to being a film critic or historian, he nonetheless included film as a noteworthy resource for providing examples of curricula beyond textbook examples. His unpublished nonfiction includes explanations of such examples in Westerns directed by John Ford, Howard Hawks and Anthony Mann.

In Pursuit by Herman W. Hansen

ONLY ONE SURVIVED

KYLEIGH MCCLOUD

A PALE-PINK glove lay on the murky Powder River embankment almost covered with dark-brown sand that could pass for gunpowder. Blaze's heart gathered speed as he snatched up the orphaned kid glove. He examined the wet, dirty glove for its missing owner along the shoreline. Men and women's clothes, hats, and unmentionables floated on the lazy, trickling river, or lay strewn about the banks, but no sign of people. He tucked the wayward glove inside his saddlebag as he rode up river toward Old Fort Reno and scanned the rugged landscape. The floating trail of clothes extended southward.

As midday passed, Blaze removed his duster and tied it with his bedroll, continuing his search for the glove's missing owner. The clothing trail became sparse. He and his blue roan rode another ten miles when lingering smoke cloyed the air. His stomach rebelled. "If anyone survived, they better count their blessings."

Blaze urged Storm on, despite the horse's protests. His eyes watered and nose burned at the acrid aroma growing stronger the closer he traveled toward the source. Ahead lay a battered trunk—lid smashed with wood splinters lined like rows of jagged teeth. The blue roan snorted and tamped the ground.

Blaze stroked the gelding's neck and finished with a pat. "All right, boy. We'll camp here for the night."

As the sunset disappeared behind the darkened bluffs, Blaze slipped into his duster and tugged it snug. He removed the pink glove from his saddlebag and caressed the soft material. The fire crackled and popped nearby. In the glow, Blaze observed his blue roan grazing grasses along the cottonwood trees and brush. To the west, the Bighorn Mountains could be seen on the horizon. His gaze traveled to the expansive, starry sky and locked onto the clear, full moon.

Whoever he was searching for, she had to be alive. Perhaps the woman was looking at the moon, too. A shiver rippled through Blaze. Or the glove's owner might be haunting him until he laid her body to rest.

———————

DISTANT SCREAMS PIERCED the mountain air. Blaze flailed against his friend's grip as he fought to rescue his wife and daughter from the roaring Colorado River's torrents. He shouted after them. Whiskers and a velvet nose tickled his face and startled him awake. The screaming vanished. He jerked upright and ghosted the blue roan while he glanced frantically about for Ellie and Caroline.

It was only a dream.

Blaze panted and clutched the front of his duster, but the familiar U.S. Marshal star he sought for comfort was gone. The badge's absence provided the painful reminder he wasn't worthy of it anymore. He had failed his family. And he'd be damned if he let this woman die.

Storm nudged him again, and Blaze cursed. He rubbed his eyes and pinched the bridge of his nose. "All right, I'm gittin' up."

The spry gray-blue horse stole the pink glove and whirled around while Blaze attempted to reclaim the item. Each time he tried, Storm withdrew the glove just out of reach. He pursued the naughty blue roan farther into the trees. His pants and duster snagged on the brush along the way.

"Stop it," he snapped. "Give me—"

Indistinct talking carried, and Blaze stiffened at the language they spoke. Lakota Sioux. He strained an ear and discovered faint crying amongst the conversation between the Indians. His heart constricted at the possibility the glove's owner was with them. Blaze freed his Winchester rifle from the scabbard and hid behind a tree trunk with an unobstructed view of his campsite. He aimed and waited.

A small band of warriors rode followed by a prisoner dragged by a rope. Blaze slowed his breathing. The half-dozen Lakota men halted. One hopped down from his horse's bare back and hovered a hand above the low embers. He glanced up at his comrades and spoke.

Blaze kneeled behind the tree trunk, rifle at the ready. He needed to find the missing woman before they did. Unless he was too late.

The warriors talked amongst themselves, and Blaze deduced the topic being about him. A woman's pleas surprised him. His stomach dropped when a young man raised a hand to her. She stammered, "I don't know where Nelly could be."

Blaze squinted for a glimpse of the woman concealed by the horses and warriors. The same man tugged on the rope, revealing a woman with disheveled straw-colored hair, and slapped her hard across the face. A shrill cry rang out as she fell to her knees. Her assailant raised a hand again.

Without thought, Blaze fired at the offender. The woman's attacker stumbled back and collapsed on the slippery embankment—water splashing.

Blaze narrowly missed a volley of bullets. He moved from behind the tree, aimed, and killed another. The others returned fire. A burning sensation made him wince, and he checked his arm, then cursed at the crimson stain on his fingers.

Burnt gunpowder obscured the air, and the war cries faded. The metallic tang of blood overpowered Blaze's senses as he huddled against the safety of his tree trunk. His heartbeat drummed in his ears. The woman's screams broke his stupor. He swiped his bloodied fingers across his duster and leaned out to return fire.

"Let me go," she shrieked.

Blaze stiffened at the salt-and-peppered hair man holding the woman hostage by her hair while pulling her toward the trees. A knife glinted in the sun, and he pressed the blade against her throat. He shouted, "Come out or I'll kill her."

"Please," the shaky woman pleaded between sobs.

Frozen, Blaze narrowed his stinging eyes and sighted on the woman's captor. Perspiration dripped from his forehead. If he fired, he risked killing or maiming her. He was still outnumbered four to one.

Nelly... you didn't come this far to fail her.

Storm whinnied and crashed through the brush toward the hostiles. Blaze seized the opportunity and rose quickly from his crouched position, firing at the Indian holding a hostage. Blood and brain matter splattered against the screaming woman. She fled down the river bank.

Steel-eyed bloodlust raged as Blaze dropped the Winchester rifle and sprinted forward with a loud growl. He yanked his Colts from his double holster just like he had done during battles in the War Between the States. If he was to die, he preferred to go down shooting. The remaining three warriors and he exchanged gunfire until one emerged.

THE GROUND CRUNCHED beneath the woman's shoes as she approached him in a blur. Blaze stood still, panting and gripping his two Colts. Bodies, ichor, and blood stained the once pristine land. When the woman spoke, he blinked until his vision cleared. He winced at the hot burn in his upper-right arm and holstered his weapons, then dared to examine the streaming blood pool.

A flesh wound. Blaze groaned. The wound would have to be taken care of later. He glanced at the distraught woman and studied her for any outward injuries. "You didn't come to harm did you, ma'am?"

"Only bruises and cuts, but they'll heal." She lifted her battered hands, and Blaze claimed the knife her assailant no longer needed, cutting her free. He observed her vivid green eyes. A darker green color outlined an emerald green with flecks of gold dotted throughout them. Their uniqueness captivated him. The woman rubbed her rope-burned, raw wrists. "Thank you for rescuing me from those savages."

"Ma'am, are you sure you're fine?"

She appeared to stare past him, and Blaze glanced over his shoulder, discovering his blue roan with the pink glove. The stranger marched toward Storm and retrieved the dangling object from his mouth. She crushed the kid glove inside a small fist and whispered, "Nelly."

Blaze reclaimed his Stetson off the ground and joined her. Tears beaded on the woman's thick eyelashes and trickled down her sunburned face. He pressed the hat against his chest. With the gunshots, they needed to move. He clasped a large hand over hers. "I'm sorry, but it's best not to linger any longer, or the others will be upon us before sundown."

Amid the previous chaos, the Indians' horses had fled. Blaze cursed silently. Riding double would slow them, but they had no choice. He helped the stranger into the worn saddle, and when he sat behind her, she squeaked.

The woman started to shiver.

"Here." Blaze grabbed his blanket from behind and draped it over her shoulders.

"Thank you, Mister...?" The woman seemed to lean toward the river. She tugged the woolen blanket closer.

"Blaze Sutton. And this is Storm."

"Annabelle Walker. But please call me Belle. It's only right, considering the circumstances."

Blaze urged Storm on, and they rode along the tree line as best as they could. His gelding navigated the uneven terrain with sure footing. Belle's head nodded forward, and then she'd jerk back as if to stop herself from sleeping. He cleared his throat. "When's the last time you've slept?"

"Not since I lost the life I had because of my father and husband's hare-brained business scheme to wash the miners." Belle spat out the words in a venomous tone.

Off in the distance, Blaze spotted wispy smoke and blackened remnants of what had once been prairie wagons. The stench of death grew stronger as they neared the gruesome scene. He stopped Storm and surveyed the men's bodies and parts strewn about. If any had survived the massacre, scavengers had finished them. Women were taken as captives he surmised.

Belle gagged. "I'm gonna be sick."

Blaze helped her down, and she staggered a few feet then retched. He dismounted and led Storm over to her. "I'm sorry for your loss. Is this where you saw Nelly last?"

Belle nodded and vomited again, coughing after she finished. Blaze fetched his canteen and offered it. She accepted the water with a weak smile and drank while Blaze noted her pallor. His lips pursed at the painful reminder of when Ellie was expecting their child. "You're in the family way, ain't ya?"

Water dribbled down Belle's chin, and she swiped at the droplets with a tattered sleeve. She returned the canteen and turned away. Her gaze rested on the bluff where Fort Reno overlooked. She sniffled.

"My little sister didn't survive after I pushed her in the river beneath the wagon did she? I-I-I thought maybe if those savages thought she was dead that they'd leave her be."

"We'll keep looking," Blaze replied grimly. When Belle gazed at him, eyes dewy, he added, "There's still hope. Perhaps she escaped for the trees or to the fort. Wherever she is, I promise ya, we'll find her."

YOU FOOL. WHAT'D you do that for? The admonishment swirled about Blaze's head hours after he and Belle returned to their search for Nelly. He shouldn't have made a promise he didn't have control over the results. Afternoon waned into early evening with a futile search at the fort and surrounding area. Temperatures dropped. Long shadows began to engulf the valley. He prayed Nelly had the wits to stave off hypothermia.

When Belle's teeth chattered, Blaze tugged on the reins, and Storm halted. She straightened up in the saddle and stuttered, "What are you doing? It's still plenty of daylight left to look for my sister."

"You're freezing." Blaze dismounted and offered a hand. "And my horse is tired, as are you. Now, let's get you warmed up and well-rested, and we'll start fresh in the morning."

"No! You don't understand. I need to find her," Belle exclaimed. Darkened green eyes narrowed into slits as her chin jutted out. She shivered and pulled her blanket closer. Blaze dropped his hand at his side and struggled to not cuss in front of her.

Out of habit, Blaze spoke in a stern voice. "I understand. But you aren't in the position to demand anything at the moment, not when your health is at stake."

"Fine."

The obstinate woman fumbled as she tried to swing a weary leg over the saddle and finally did after several attempts. Blaze reached to help her down. But she hopped down instead and stumbled like a newborn foal. He caught her when she almost fell.

"I'll look for my little sister myself," Belle snapped as she pushed him away.

Blaze clenched his jaw as Belle marched off. He caught a glimpse of brown fur waddling through the trees. Blaze reached for his rifle and hollered at her, "Stop! Don't move."

When she didn't, Blaze dropped Storm's reins and sprinted after her. He grabbed Belle's wrist and jerked her to a stop. She yanked her arm but couldn't free herself from his tight grip, then flailed against him. "Leave me alone."

"Be quiet. There's a grizzly coming." Blaze hissed. His heart thundered at facing the enormous beast. He nudged Belle toward his horse. "Hurry, before Storm takes off."

The pair fled to where the blue roan waited. Just after Blaze helped Belle atop Storm, the grizzly bear emerged from the woods and ambled toward the Powder River. A fish slapped the water's surface. The humans' gazes locked on each other, and Blaze pressed a finger against his mouth. Holding the rifle in one hand, he grasped onto the reins with the other and led them into the trees while the giant bear fished.

With them out of temporary harm's way, Blaze stopped Storm and placed the Winchester in its scabbard. Then they rode, putting distance between them and the grizzly bear.

Questions assaulted his mind. As his hope diminished for finding Nelly in this vast wilderness, he dared not admit Belle might be right. If her little sister didn't meet her maker with the Lakota, hypothermia or wildlife would finish her. Their brush with the bear had reminded him of the many dangers lurking about in Montana Territory.

DESPITE THE FIRE, Blaze witnessed Belle shivering and scooting closer to the red-orange flames. He suspected her chill had more to do with her missing sister. The Winchester rifle beside him, he leaned back against Storm's saddle and pulled the brim of his hat over his eyes. "It's late. You best get some shuteye."

Blaze folded his arms across his battle-scarred chest. His injured arm ached, and he worried about infection after ignoring his flesh wound all day before tending to it.

The woolen blanket rustled several times like Belle was fidgeting. Grasses rasped together in the cold breeze. Distant lonesome howls mingled with the coyote's nighttime cacophony in the trees behind their campsite. Still, Belle continued to fidget.

"There somethin' you wanna ask me?" Blaze asked. He pushed up his Stetson and met her inquisitive gaze. Her eyes reflected the flames dancing.

"Why aren't you a lawman?"

Blaze straightened with a stretch and a yawn. He rummaged through the pocket of his torn duster and clasped his hand around the familiar badge. His grip tightened until the object bit into his palm. A lump clogged in his throat. Being a marshal seemed like another lifetime ago.

"I'm not worthy of the badge anymore. Not after what happened...," he finally said below a whisper.

"You saved me. I don't know many men who could have accomplished what you did with being outnumbered." Belle revealed the dirty pink glove. "To be honest, I don't deserve to be saved. I lied about how my little sister ended up in the river."

Blaze narrowed his eyes, reached for the rifle, and tossed the U.S. Marshal badge at her feet. If he hadn't been a fool, would he have thought about the possibility of being on a wild goose chase? He tensed. The flickering flames showed glistening tears as Belle retrieved the item. Her thumb swiped over the metal, and she stared at the etched words.

"If I can't save your sister... then I'm not worthy enough to wear that badge of honor and will turn it in."

"You are. I've never seen a man more determined to save me, even if it meant losing your life. Does it mean my life isn't worth as much as my little sister's?"

"No, of course not." Blaze watched the kid glove dangling from Belle's hand. She was right. He hadn't thought about the importance of saving her, for he had been too focused on finding the glove's owner.

Belle rose and closed the gap between them. She offered the pink glove, and Blaze gently tugged it from her delicate fingers. He traced the stitching and then the two buttons. Tears streamed down her face, and her voice grew high-pitched. "Nelly had given me the pink gloves as a birthday present. And now it might be the last thing I have from her."

Blaze clasped onto her icy hands. The tension in his body dissipated. "I think tomorrow we should ride to Fort Phil Kearny and request help."

Belle agreed and freed her hands. She laid the kid glove aside and leaned forward, pinning the U.S. Marshal star on Blaze's duster. When Blaze tried to protest, she pressed a finger against his chapped lips and patted the badge. "You are more than worthy,"

"When I became a marshal, I didn't consider how it might affect my family. That the outlaws I pursued like prey might turn into the hunters. And that's how I lost —"

A sharp crack interrupted. Blaze readied his rifle as he quickly stood, aiming at the noise's source. "Who's there?"

His heart pounded. Had another bear come, or had the remaining Lakota Sioux warriors tracked them here? A jackrabbit darted out from the trees, and Belle screamed at the same time Blaze fired. The rabbit squealed and collapsed in the grass. He strode over to the rabbit's lifeless body and paused, then raised his rifle again. Seconds stretched into minutes as he waited and observed.

Blaze's skin prickled at an eerie hoot. He lifted his rifle and fired at the brilliant nighttime sky. "Come out, whoever you are. Or I'll fire at ya."

A woman's shrill voice shouted, "Please, don't."

Blaze continued to aim, far too many people had fallen for a harmless woman's act. With how brutal the Indian attack on the wagon train was, he found the idea of Nelly being alive on her own in the frontier difficult. The ground crunched with hastened footsteps. Belle stopped beside him and cupped her mouth, "Nelly? Is that you?"

"Belle?" the stranger's voice asked. A figure approached them, the flames uncovering a petite woman nearly identical to Belle in appearances. The woman sprinted toward them and exclaimed, "Annabelle!"

Blaze lowered his gun as the two women met each other and embraced. They had found Nelly, or rather, she had found them. He watched them with a wary eye. The sisters stepped back, examined, and patted each other, then hugged again. Upon his scrutiny, Nelly appeared to be tidy. Too tidy for surviving an attack and being on her own.

Uneasiness niggled at Blaze at the sudden appearance at their campsite. He raised his rifle at Nelly. When the two women's eyes widened, he whispered, "How many are there?"

"Blaze, what are you doing?" Belle screamed.

"Answer me," Blaze shouted. A glimpse of movement in the trees caught his attention, and he fired at the moving target.

Nelly lunged and fought to wrest the Winchester rifle from him, but she was no match for his height and build. He shoved her, and she tumbled to the ground while Belle went to her aid. A battle cry pierced the night, and a man dashed toward them—arrow drawn. Blaze squeezed the trigger, felling the man while the drawn arrow soared to the clouds.

"You'll never kill them all. This is their land," Nelly said in a frosty tone.

Blaze targeted her and ordered Belle to fetch handcuffs from his saddlebag. She remained frozen at her sister's side. He pleaded, "Please. If you want Nelly to live, we've got to leave now."

Blocking his view from Nelly, Belle rose slower than Blaze expected and continued to stare at him. His heart dropped into his stomach. Sparks exploded and gunfire exchanged. The pink glove flew from Belle's hand and landed onto the ground covered in blood spatter.

Only one survived.

—North Dakota Native Kyleigh McCloud lives in Minnesota with her husband and rescue cat. Writing has always been in her blood. As a result, she attended Minnesota State University Moorhead and graduated with a BS in Mass Communications, emphasis in Print Journalism.

While Kyleigh loves to read a variety of genres, her favorite is historical romance. She has always felt drawn to the 1800s time period. The Little House on the Prairie *series introduced her to this era when she was in fifth grade. Ever since, Kyleigh has admired the people's tenacity to survive back then. She and her husband love traveling the Midwest to visit historical sites.*

Aside from writing westerns, Kyleigh writes contemporary women's fiction and historical fiction. She has multiple short stories published in various anthologies and also has two holiday novellas. To follow Kyleigh's writing journey, check her website www.kyleighmccloud.com, or follow her at www. facebook.com/authorkyleighmccloud.

HAT CREEK

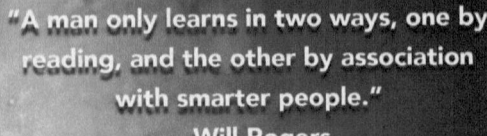

"A man only learns in two ways, one by
reading, and the other by association
with smarter people."
—Will Rogers

WILL ROGERS
MEDALLION

RECOGNIZING EXCELLENCE IN WESTERN MEDIA AND STORYTELLING AND COWBOY POETRY

www.willrogersmedallionaward.net

AN EPIC JOURNEY
OF RESILIENCE, HONOR,
AND THE RELENTLESS
PURSUIT OF JUSTICE.

As the trusted lieutenant of the infamous Geronimo, Chato's days are painted in the hues of raid and revolt until personal tragedy strikes when his family are taken into slavery in Mexico. Hoping to secure their release, Chato strikes a deal to aid the U.S. Army in maintaining peace with his people. But when Geronimo denounces him as a traitor and departs, all hope for Chato's family flees with him. Forsaken by his former brothers-in-arms, Chato vows to hunt down the renegades himself, becoming a beacon of the Chiricahua peace faction clinging to reservation life in the process.

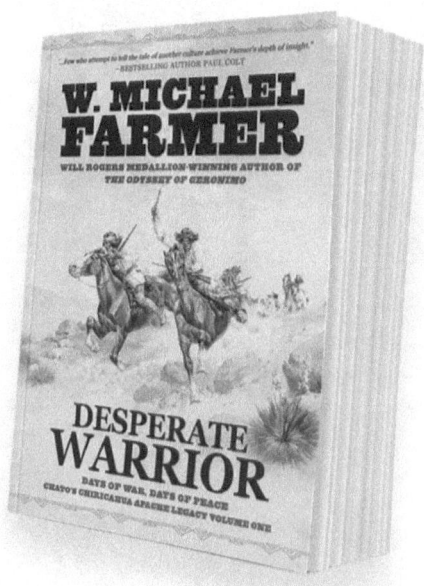

"... Few who attempt to tell the tale of another culture achieve Farmer's depth of insight."

—Bestselling Western author Paul Colt

Don't Miss W. Michael Farmer's other award-winning novels from Hat Creek, including The Odyssey of Geronimo: Twenty-Three Years a Prisoner of War *and* The Iliad of Geronimo: A Song of Blood and Fire. *Available at your favorite local bookseller*

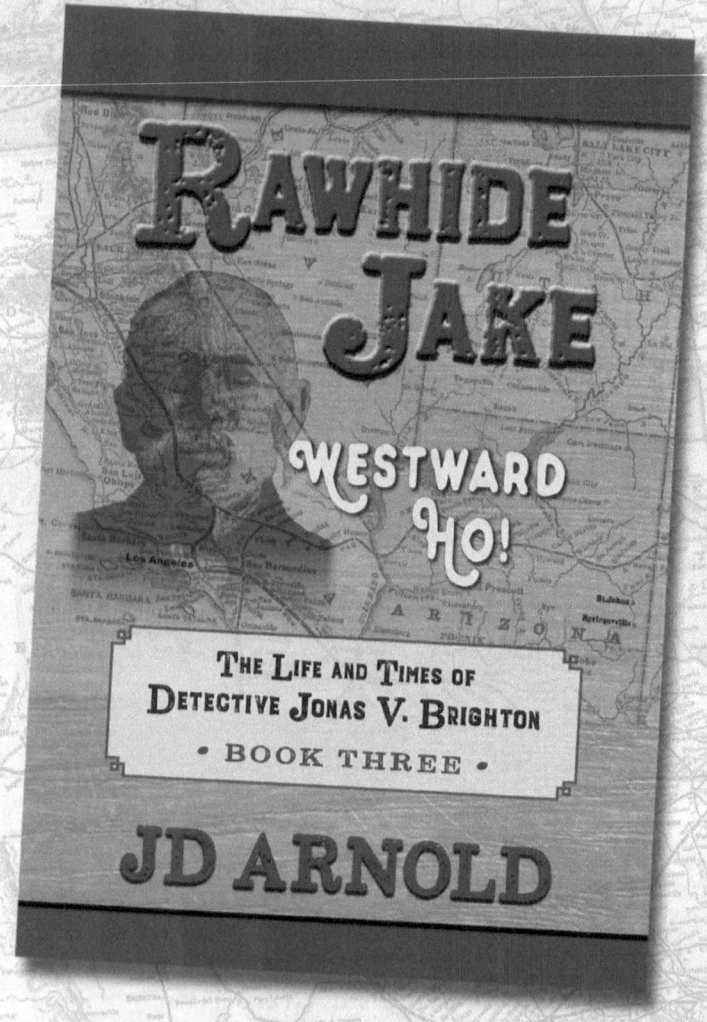

www.ingramcontent.com/pod-product-compliance
Lightning Source LLC
Chambersburg PA
CBHW050835180626
46814CB00004B/1634